Onesimus
Flight to
Exceptional

From Ordinary to Extra Ordinary
Updated 10/1/21

_____by_____
DR. ROBBIE E. SMITH

Description

Onesimus was an ordinary man who lived during the time the Romans had control over the Jewish nation. He woke up every morning and did the bidding of his master. But Onesimus had a secret. He wanted to change his life. He knew that a mundane life was not for him, but he did not know how to change his stars.

He had hope, the kind that you grab onto when you have a great idea. As he clings to his idea, he runs away. It was the big city that would offer him the impossible. So, he ran away from his master, Philemon, and headed to Rome. Thus, he started his journey from ordinary to extraordinary.

Additional Information

This book is designed for three purposes:

- It can be used in a bible study group. It includes discussions, which are thought-provoking, and it has study questions.

- It includes the author's storytelling feature to allow you to look deeper into the thoughts of the Apostle Paul, Philemon, and Onesimus.

- It is also created for personal study.

I ask you a question: Do you want to change your life? Then you have chosen the right book that will reveal to you how to become extraordinary.

Contents

PART TWO

Acknowledgments

<u>Family</u>:
I want to acknowledge my entire family for their dedication to the work of our Lord and Savior, Jesus Christ. It is through their lives and their support that I was able to draft this book: Mack and Mary Rowland, Pamela Smith, Mack Rowland, Jr. And to my big brother, Gregory Smith, thank you for your support and believing in me as the Holy Spirit led me to write this book.

<u>To The Reader</u>:
May you find where you are and be determined to go from ordinary to extraordinary.

Special Instructions

There is a great deal of detail about Onesimus' life that the bible did not include. So that we can get a closer view of his life, I will add information that I believe will give us a clear picture of his life. Remember, when you see the words **"my version**," the author has added to the story to fill in the missing pieces of Onesimus' life.

I also included the scriptures from the book of Philemon so that you can see where the bible ends and my creativity began.

Chapter One

Set Your Mind To Hope

From the time we are toddlers, we are told we can become anyone if we put our minds towards it. Those words sound wonderful in the ears of a child; why it sounds wonderful in the ears of an adult. I ask you, **"Can a man change** himself? Can he become what his heart desires?"

I say, **"Yes, he can**." We have read books and seen famous people on television who have lost hundreds of pounds or walked across America to support a change and or to make one. You may even know people who became doctors and lawyers, senators, governors, and so forth. The ability to do something starts in the heart of the person, but what about a slave!

A slave is not sent to school to learn to read and write; his soul purpose in life is to work for his master. And most people during the times of the Apostles were slaves, and they did not have hope for a brighter future.

The Hebrew interpretation of hope supplies a picture of what happens when a person hopes. The word "hope" is Tikvah. Strong's definition defines it as a cord, expectation, and hope. The Hebrew root: kavah, which implies "to bind together, collect; to expect: - tarry, wait (for, on, upon) (1)

Therefore, hope is something one can grab hold of and then cling to it. Hope is not out of reach; it is obtainable. One can expect to obtain, even though one may have to wait for, wait on or wait upon the manifestation. If you are willing to tarry, the thing that you hope is what you are clinging to. Hold on with both hands as you wait upon the Lord Jesus Christ to bless you in that specific area of your life.

The story of Onesimus is a remarkable story about a slave who had hope that his life would change. He ran away from his master and thus started the journey of the life of Onesimus.

There is so much information about Onesimus' life that remains a mystery to us. Therefore, I have added my imagination to his story to fill in the missing information. Remember, when you see the words "**my version,**" it is me [the author] adding her additional details to round out the story.

My version will give you a fuller insight to carry the story further. The original scriptures from the book of Philemon are included so that you can see facts from fiction.

ORDINARY PEOPLE

Now, allow me to shout out to ordinary people. Those who are not gifted to sing, dance, draw or speak poetically. Do not worry if you do not have an exceptional IQ either. These skills or talents are what the world seems to focus on the most. If you do not have an amazing talent, you fall into the ordinary category, like me, because you do not have a skill that entertains people. For the world seeks entertainment. But you do not have to take a seat on the sidelines because your gifts and talents do not excite them.

When we look at characters in the bible, we see that most of them were ordinary people. Some were shepherds, fishermen, tent makers, and so forth. They had natural talents in the area they worked in, but there was more to them than their jobs.

Their skills or gifts came forth one day, which changed them from ordinary to extraordinary. It is essential to learn that everyone has a gift or talent. We must utilize our gift/skill towards helping other people, thus, making the world a better place. Natural talents can be learned, although God takes part in your ability to understand natural things.

If you are a Christian, your gift and or talent are crucial to the Body of Christ. We cannot allow people to devalue us. Always give thanks to God for the blessings He has imparted into you. If you understand your gift/talent, you will use them for His purpose. Your skills/talents are what make you unique from others. Use your gift/talent to glorify God. You celebrate Him as you use them because you show Him that you value the things that He has imparted into you. And you recognize that your spiritual gift(s) comes from the power on high.

SPIRITUAL VS NATURAL

Spiritual gifts are given by God, and natural talents are those gifts and or abilities you were born with or you learned them. Everyone cannot fully grasp algebra nor draw on a professional level. Still, one can be taught how to do something at the level of their understanding.

When we look at Spiritual gifts, we see they are not gifts that one is trained to do, but they are gifts given, and one simply begins to use them. They are imparted into a person by the Holy Spirit, and those gifts/talents work by the Spirit of God. When this power, from on high, electrifies the atmosphere, you can expect to see miracles of healing arise from it. William J Seymour's wife, Jennie, claimed she began to play the piano after the Holy Spirit fell upon her one night during the Azusa Revival. She professes that before her encounter with the Spirit, she had never played the piano before. (2)

AN ORDINARY SLAVE

Onesimus was an ordinary man who was born in slavery during the time of the Apostles. Onesimus dreamed of a better life. His desire became so strong that the only solution to his problem was to run away.

Let me stop right here and say that being ordinary is okay if you are satisfied with your life. This book was not written for those who are comfortable with this lifestyle, but it is for those who are frustrated. I ask you, what would you do to become more than what you are now?"

What route have you taken to fulfill that vision? Has it worked for you? Did you start with a burning desire to do something exceptional in your life? But as time went on, your fire dwelled down due to life's difficulties. Do you yet yearn to be more than who you are?

I tell you that every Christian should have that same yearning to step out of the ordinary. The desire to please God should be first in our hearts, in our speech, and our actions, and when we have done what pleases God, He will open the door for you to begin your journey.

Your hearts-desire should tell you that you are more than who you are now and more than what you have been told. There are facts, and then there is "The Truth." The Truth of God always overrides and or supersedes facts.

It does not matter where you came from, it does not matter who your parents are were, it does not matter what excuse you use against yourself or anything a man would label you as. Even if they categorize you as "no count" because you have nothing, you do not have to accept their definition of who you are. It is not the starting line that counts, but the ones who cross the finish line.

The moment you are born, you start the race, but the one who wins does not have to be the swiftest. I know that does not sound logical, but God's way operates on a higher level than ours. His thoughts are higher, and His vision sees further, and He knows all things. (3)

God can fix you and your destiny. Our Father God is a career changer. God can change your future just as He did for Abraham. Abraham was given a promise which changed his focus. He went from idol worshipping to counting the stars. God took old fearful Gideon and made him a great leader and warrior. And He took

Saul/Paul, who thought he was standing for justice, but instead was a murder of innocent Christians and made him the head apostle for the Gentiles.

The other disciples preached the gospel to the Jews. But it was Paul whom Jesus ordained to preach the gospel to the entire Gentile world. These men's lives went from ordinary to extraordinary, all because of God's grace, mercy, and anointing. God set them on fire for the gospel, and we who came afterward are encouraged by their faithfulness.

If the fire is yet burning inside you, and I am sure it is, to do important things for God, do not let it go. Bombard heaven with your prayer cries.

Repeat after me:

God, I want to serve you. Take this fire, this overwhelming desire of mine, and allow me to serve you with it. I cannot do this alone, nor will I go ahead of you. I need your help, and I need the Holy Spirit to lead and guide me.

Father give me my stars to count in the heavens, let me die of a good old age knowing that I gave out all that was in me for the Kingdom of God."

Remind God of His promise in Jeremiah 29, which is:

> For I know the plans I have for you,"
> says the LORD. They are plans for good
> and not for disaster, to give you
> a future and a hope." (Jer.29:11)

He promised you a future with hope. Continue to put your hope in the Lord, expecting that future. Life is not over with, but your mundane life is. Proclaim that you shall never be ordinary again. In the Kingdom of God, there are no ordinary people. It is filled with unique peculiar people who make up God's treasure. We are a Holy Nation, a Chosen Generation, a Royal Priesthood. (4)

God took ordinary people and made them into vessels of honor for His purpose and to give Himself glory. Tell me, "What is ordinary about God ?" Nothing, absolutely nothing. And if we are created in His image and His likeness, and the Holy Spirit lives inside us, we have become new creatures in Christ? We are no longer ordinary but unique in all aspects.

CREATION

One major thing that God has done is that He

17

has created the heavens and the earth. He populated the sky as well as the earth with beautiful things. And then God made humanity. He wants us to have everything we need in life, and He wants us to enjoy the beauty that He put into this world.

Therefore, no matter where you look, you will see God. He is seen in the skies, the land, and the seas. Our responsibility in the garden and even after the fall is to believe God exists, love Him, worship Him, keep His commandments, and have dominion over everything upon the earth.

Everything in the garden was created for us and not us being created for the garden. For we have dominion over the earth and every living thing, then we have dominion over ourselves. You have power, authority, and control over the earth.

Remember these three statements; they will keep you focused:

- Use your **God-given power** to change your life by faith.

- Use your **authority to speak** against any negativity that tries to overtake you and destroy the desire you hold inside.

- Use your **godly wisdom** to recognize who is working against you and resist evil.

If you ask, how do I know when to use my....power, authority, and wisdom, I say use it now! The devil has come to kill, steal, and destroy what The Word/Jesus Christ has given you. Evil says to hate and believe in an eye-for-an-eye, but The Word says, "surrender, stand firm, have faith, and above all **TRUST** in the Lord your God.

MAINTAIN DOMINION

There is <u>work to be done</u> by us to keep the authority God has given us. You need God's power to have dominion and to keep it. There is a fight going on, so do not be deceived. The devil is doing everything he can to take your power away from you.

Yet God has given you everything you need to become to defeat him and to become extraordinary. He placed it in you the moment He adopted you and called you one of His children. When the Holy Spirit created you a new spirit, He imparted all the Zoe life you will ever need. If you do not believe it, then how will you ever receive the power it contains? You cannot receive your new life without believing that God exists.

You cannot flow in the anointing that exists in a Zoe life if you do not accept Jesus Christ as your Savior. Therefore, your new life will sit dormant until you activate it with your faith.

Now, look at yourself. God has put beauty and worth into you, just as He did with the heavens. You have gifts and talents, and your smile is captivating to all who have the pleasure of experiencing it.

You are a unique specimen called man, and your character and personality are from God. You bless everyone in your world by your touch and the words that you speak. Some gifts are not easily recognizable, especially those gifts that do not manifest themselves in a dramatic way.

Dramatic gifts are gifts like singing, drawing, or dancing. Your gift may not catch the eye of the world, but that does not mean it is not working. You are a vessel of honor, made by the potter's hand. He called you forth before the foundation of the world to be one of His elects. (5) Yes, He has given you everything pertaining to life and godliness. (6)

The word everything implies "all manner of," and the word life refers to a Zoe life, and the word godliness suggests holiness. Thus, God has placed into you all manner of good and holy things, the entire package of Zoe life, which makes you bless. If you have these things and you cannot see them operating, then it is up to you to surrender to the leading of the Holy Spirit. He will help you to put things in order, according to God's standard of holiness.

Yes, when you allow yourself to be trained in godliness, you find benefits, blessings, and abundance coming to you. The design is already cut for you. It is a precut design with a twist. There is only one pattern, but trillions of designs are coming forth from that one pattern. Jesus' lifestyle is the precut pattern, but it is the Holy Spirit that fashions each piece into its uniqueness.

Questions:

• Do you yet feel ordinary?(Read: Gen 1:27, 5:1; Deu 4:32; Eph 4:24)

• Do you know what your piece is designed to do? (Read: 1 Cor 12; Luk 13:12; Jhn 1:42; Rom 1:7; Gal 1:6; 1 Cor 1:25-27)

• Can you have a pattern without material, or can you make a dress without the thread? (Read: 1 Cor 12:17; Isa 64:8; Jer 18:4; Jhn 9:11)

CHAPTER TWO

CONSIDER HIS WORDS

Now consider what God says about you: He tells us we are His children, and the Holy Spirit confirms it. (7) Those who become children of God are those who believe in the Son of God by faith. (8) And those who are children of God were born again; therefore, your new identity entitles you to receive the blessings that were set in the new covenant. (9) And those known as children of God are the ones whom God listens for and answers. (10)

God's children are blessed going in and going out. (11) The Holy Spirit, the comforter, will dwell inside each believer forever. He will lead and guide those believers to all truth. (12) What truths are those? Truths about Jesus Christ, those about God, and those things you need to know about you. And when the world tries to tell you about Jesus, God, or yourself, He will always redirect you back to God's Words (The Bible). He will give you **The Truth** about every area of your life, and He will be your guide, for He is an excellent guide.

And how does the Holy Spirit guides:

- He reveals the way by leading, instructing, or advising. (Read Matt 10:19)

- He reminds you of the standard that God sets. (Read Jhn 14:26; 2 Pe 1:21)

Now I tell you that signs and wonders follow the believers. (13) That same power that raised Christ from the grave is the same power that lives in the true believer. (14 Allow that power to work in you; it will break every chain.

Prayer:
Those that are oppressed, I call you out of those things which confuses your mind, place burden upon you from power or authority that abuses you in the Name of Jesus! You are no longer an ordinary person but an extra ordinary man/woman in Christ. Receive the blessings of life that Christ has made accessible to you.

Questions:

- What promises of God do you rely on upon in times of trouble? (Read: Phil 4:19; Isa 40:31; Matt 11:28-30)

- What has hope in the Lord done for you?   (Read: 1 Pe 1:3; Acts 8:22)

- Make a list of five promises of God. Make them personal and post them where   you can see them every day.

CHAPTER THREE

SMALL BEGINNINGS

Onesimus was an ordinary man who lived during the time the Roman had control over the Jewish nation. He woke up every morning and did the bidding of his master. He may have fetched the water from the river or started the fires so someone could make breakfast. He may have been assigned to feed and water the animals or clean out their stalls or work in the field. Still, whatever he was given to do, it was ordinary, day-to-day chores assigned by his master or his master's overseer. If they told him to go or to come, he obeyed their every command.

Can you identify with Onesimus as a slave? In this context, I am referring to being a slave to the routine of your life. Today, we can see that you can become a slave to something. Are you a slave to something, or are you the dominant one? If you are not the slave, then you are the one making slaves out of others. There are other things we do that make a person a slave, such as drugs, alcohol, or drinking. People pleasing, desiring control, and being caught up in material things are some more examples of how you can become bound. You wake up every morning with the same routine, you wash your faces and brush your teeth, you fix breakfast, kiss your spouse goodbye. Then you take the kids to school, go to work, serve your boss, and try to live up to people's expectations. You return home, have dinner, watch a little television, and then go to bed. Twice a week, you may attend church service, but overall, NOTHING major happens. And each moment or every minute, your dreams lie dormant, and time is slipping away.

You are a twisted mess, for you are physically bound, or you are spiritually dull to the point you suppress the fire that wants to ignite inside you. You have painted yourself a dark world without hope.

Life does not have to be this way, for Jesus said he has come that you might have life…life more abundantly. (15) The life Jesus refers to is "Zoe life." When one has Zoe life, they have the God kind of life; it is full of love, joy, power, and abilities. (16)

Thayer's Greek Lexicon says that a Zoe life is: "the state of one who is possessed of vitality or is animate." So, Jesus promises life to have liveliness, vigor, and strength. (17) If not, one must check to see what prevents this Zoe life from reproducing itself in you.

Christ promises an abundant life, which is a Zoe life, and we know he keeps his word, and then we must pray to God, asking Him to help us. He will answer your prayer and show you those things blocking you from a Zoe life in Him. Examine yourself against the Word and ask yourself, "Do I live a life that is pleasing to God, or do I please myself?" Now focus for a few minutes on those things that are being unveiled to you.

REQUIRED FAITH

Almost everything given to you by God requires faith. Just five little letters of little significance until you put them together to form a word that God will answer. Did you ever stop to think that faith gives you influence into the supernatural? Your confidence in Jesus gets the attention of God...The God of the Universe. Faith draws Him to you, and it is faith that causes Him to respond to your request.

Remember this moto of faith:

- ☐ Faith Arises Inside Trouble Hearts.

- ☐ Faith Adheres Itself Through Horrendousness Times

- ☐ Faith Advocates Inwardly /out-wardly Through Tough Situations

27

When you have faith in the promises of God, those promises will begin to manifest them. You must believe that there is a Zoe life and that it is yours to have. For some of you, it may take fasting and praying and studying the Word of God to have the faith to BELIVE IT. For we know that faith cometh by hearing and hearing the Word of God. (18)

Read the Word and then speak the Word out so you can hear it. The opportunity is yours, choose and believe in Him. Jesus said, "The Kingdom of God is at hand," meaning it is now available, so exercise your faith and grab it. Cling to that until it unfolds before your eyes.

Questions:

- What has enslaved you?

- What does your life reveal to you?

- Is it ordinary or extraordinary?

- How would you want Zoe life
  to work in your life?

CHAPTER FOUR

OWNERSHIP:

Onesimus was a slave, which means he belonged to someone. You would have to agree that a slave's life is the lowest form of life for a human being. If you had to start there in life as a slave, you started off owning nothing, not even the clothes on your back. Everything would be provided for you by your master. In other words, whatever his plans were for your life, it is what you became, and you did whatever they asked of you, regardless of how you felt about it. If you were really lucky, you would begin to enjoy what you were assigned to do.

In Onesimus' time and even in the time of slavery in America, slaves were beaten when they did not perform well. Their hopes and dreams did not matter to the person who owned them. The only thing that mattered was pleasing the master by obeying him. A slave could only look forward to getting up the following day and doing his chores.

This was all Onesimus had to look forward to, a life of enslavement, a life of bitter bondage, with no means of escaping the lot given to him. It is obvious that Onesimus did not have a Zoe life in Christ Jesus which is why he ran away.

THE SECRET

But Onesimus had a secret. He wanted more than what had been handed him in life. The life that encompassed him was not enough. I imagine there were nights when he would look up at the stars and wonder about other cities. He probably dreamed that something wonderful was out there waiting for him, but he would have to go after it.

He believed that if he could find it, it would set him free from his mundane life. He needed to leave Colossae and find a better life for himself even though everything around him was screaming, "Philemon will never let you go."

I could picture that there were times when he got anxious about his destiny. He probably thought and planned a thousand ways of how to escape. He needed a full-proof plan, but something seemed to pull him back, and he would let that opportunity slip through his fingers.

ANXIOUSNESS

Anxiousness can be a slave master too. It makes you review a thing over and over in your mind. You try to turn it off for a moment, but somehow you go right back to it until anxiousness consumes you.

Escaping Colossae was the catalyst for Onesimus' anxiousness. Soon he could not hear anything around him because he was driven with the one thought, "How Can I Escape."

If you have been anxious before, you have experienced the negative words that can roll around in your mind. Maybe you rehearse what others have said to you: "You will never make it out there." Or did you convince yourself that the competition is too stiff? Here is a good one; you told yourself that you were not qualified, especially after comparing yourself with a more successful person.

Did someone tell you that you will amount to nothing? Were you told you are too tall, short, dark, light, small, fat, or skinny? All these things cause one to become anxious and fearful, and that will cause you to see yourself of less value. Maybe you said to yourself, "I do not have the proper education, I cannot read well, I do not possess the skills necessary to get the job I want." Whatever Satan whispered in your ear or however he used others to speak into your soul…those words entrapped you and made you a hostage.

These thoughts entangle you and confuse you the more you dwell upon them. Satan is the expert on lying. He wants to hold you hostage. He waits and watches for any sign of weakness, and then he pounces on you.

If you agree that this is where you are, then you are standing in Onesimus' sandals. There is a slim chance of making changes to your destiny on your own, but there are a few who do, but most ordinary people stay ordinary. Even if you make it, you will never be as successful nor fulfilled until you allow Jesus to come into your heart. With God, all things are possible. (19)

I would also add, not only are all things possible, but the possibilities in God will include **Zoe's life**, which is full of joy, peace, strength, and animation. God will choose the right path for you, and He will have the Holy Spirit place you into The Body of Christ. Rest assured, wherever He put you; it will be the perfect fit.

Now that we have found where you are, the next question is, what are you going to do about it? Your life can become more meaningful. Consider Elisha's life. It is an excellent example because his life changed suddenly. When Elijah placed his mantel upon Elisha, his life changed that day. (20) It changed because Elisha decided to follow the man of God. Therefore, he went from ordinary to extraordinary in a matter of seconds.

There is another young man we should consider discussing, and that is king David's son Absalom. This young man's sister, Tara, was raped by her half-brother, and king David did not do anything about the incident. Absalom became so anxious that he sought out a plan to kill his brother, and he also devised a plan to take over his father's kingdom. (21) In the end, Absalom was trapped by his long hair in a tree, and there he died. We will never know what his life could have been because he did not seek God for a solution.

And all things begin with God and shall end with Him; since He is Omniscient: all-knowing, Omnipotent: all-powerful, and Omnipresent: He is present everywhere. If you can accept this, then allow God to do the impossible for you. Ask Him for what you are hoping for, continuing with prayer, meditating, and fasting. Live each day with the expectation that what you desire may come today and watch Him work it out. If you put your trust in Him, all anxiousness will leave.

When we have a problem, we try to solve it, and that is what Onesimus did. He believed the only way to change his life was to run away. I visualize Onesimus planning his escape for midnight. He rose early, grabbed his bag, and he ran as fast as he could, but not without looking back to see if he was being followed.

Questions:

- Do you have a secret that is building up anxiousness inside you? (Read: Phil 4:6)

- Have you sought God about it through prayer? (Read: Isa 55:6)

- Are you willing to wait on The Lord? (Read: Isa 30:18; Zep 3:8)

CHAPTER FIVE

RUNNING AWAY

Onesimus ran away from his master, Philemon. Can you see him getting up in the middle of the night, grabbing bread and water, and taking off? Or maybe he was in the field working, and when the overseer was not looking, he slipped away.

Many theologians believe that Onesimus stole from his master before running. If so, then he stole something that he could easily carry. It would be something he could trade for food or maybe to exchange for money in order to survive in Rome, which is where he was headed.

How would one make it on the road? There are 1311.71459 miles between Colossae and Rome. (22) That is a lot of miles to travel on your own without a horse or camel or a mule. He had to face the weather. He had to look for food and keep away from wild animals. Let us not forget thieves, slave traders, Roman soldiers who could overtake him and Philemon's men who would be looking for him.

I doubt Onesimus thought about how he would make a living in the big city. He was too anxious to worry about anything except getting there. But let us look at the odds that were also against him. What did Rome have to offer another illiterate slave who had nothing to offer in skill or abilities? There were thousands of slaves in Rome at that time. Did that city really need another slave that had nothing of value to contribute to its growth?

We can see that anxiousness can cause a man to make bad decisions. Onesimus was also an anxious man. He worried about how to escape, and he feared that he would be a slave forever...stuck in a mundane life that would cut off his chance for a better future. He looked at his life as if he had a one-sided coin. That coin told him what Rome would offer him once he arrived, but not how he would survive once he got there.

When he allowed his anxiousness to take control of him, it was impossible to think clearly about the disadvantages that Rome would demand of him. And whatever Onesimus stole from his master, he did not consider the fact that it would not be enough to sustain him for very long?

SAUL AND JUDAS

Many failed because they made quick decisions due to being anxious. There are two specific men in the bible who were anxious, King Saul and Judas Iscariot. King Saul became worried when his men began to slip away from the battle at

Gilgal. They were waiting for the prophet Samuel to come to make the sacrifice.

After eight days of waiting, Samuel had not arrived. King Saul became so anxious that he took matters into his own hands. He called for the sacrifice of the burnt offering, which they needed to have performed before fighting with the Amalekites. King Saul was not a priest and therefore had no authority to make the sacrifice, but he made the sacrifice as if he was a priest. This act of rebellion caused him to lose the kingship that God had given him. (23)

And look at Judas Iscariot's life; we see he was anxious for Jesus to overthrow the Romans. He believed that Jesus would set up His Kingdom on earth. As he watched and listened, he came to realize that Jesus had a different plan. It made him so annoyed that he went out and betrayed Jesus for thirty pieces of silver. (24)

DISTORTING THE FUTURE

Why do we run away from things? When we run away from a difficult situation, we are distorting our future. Our future becomes distorted because the issue has not been solved, and thus our future will surely suffer from it. While the problem continues to exist in our hearts and minds, it will affect our thinking. And if our thinking stays distorted, we are not free to make good decisions for our future.

Onesimus ran to Rome because he thought the big city had much to offer him. Whatever was inside the walls of that great city, it called for him. He was convinced a bright future was waiting for him there.

Why We Run From Things:

1. We do not truly know how to change our destiny while remaining in that situation.

2. One's destiny is not necessarily based on a physical location.

3. We are not willing to face our situation the right way.

4. We are non-confrontational; therefore, our anxious thinking takes over, and the worry of our anxiousness attacks our minds. And then fear takes over, and it tells us to run.

5. We do not carry our burdens and desires to the Lord.

God never intended for you to do anything on your own. If you could balance goodness and greatness by yourself, you would not need a Savior.

Have you ever fought for a title or position, and once you had it, you found it enjoyable only for a fleeting moment. And some people believe that a new location is the only answer to the change they are looking for. Locations are necessary, but only if the person has tried to fix the root problem before leaving. Most problems can be resolved if one does not run. It is rare that one will need to move to a safe location after trying to resolve an issue.

Questions:

- Have you ever been anxious about something?

- Did your anxiousness get you in trouble like it did King Saul and Judas?

- How did you resolve your problem? God will zone in on your shortcomings and then work out a plan that is tailor-made for you. (Read: 2 Cor 12:90)

CHAPTER SIX

IDENTIFY THE PROBLEM

If we do not recognize where we are, how can we correct and or fix the problem so that you can move forward? We must find where we are and realize that we need God's help.

If life is going to change for you, you must be willing to fight for that change. I am not talking about street fighting with your bare knuckles or like a boxer who is trapped on the ropes. The Holy Spirit will take you from where you are and <u>work inwardly</u> to pull your assets outward. As a willing vessel, you will see Him working through you, and so will others.

Be truthful with yourself, and then make amends with God for not turning to Him first. Ask God to help you with that situation. One thing you must learn and remember about God, He is always available. He waits for you to welcome

Him into your fight. <u>When you get it right with Him</u>, then you can expect to change your stars. This is a heart issue, my friend because God is the only one who can change a tare/weed into wheat.

While you wait to see the salvation of the Lord, you can:

1. Read the Word of God.

2. Make confessions from your favorite scriptures.

3. You can set definite times throughout your day where you will fellowship with the Father.

You must do these things as you wait on the Lord. Until your heart and spirit line up with the Word of God, faith cannot take you over, neither will looks or talent. A true change comes from surrendering to the Holy Spirit. He is the one that will tell you what He hears from the Father. Onesimus needs a guide…The Holy Spirit.

MISGUIDED ONESIMUS

I am sure Onesimus thought a bigger city would give him this life-changing experience. The city could only offer another slave a temporary place to hide from his master.

Without a livelihood and talent, Onesimus was a faceless body in the market square. The big city may be able to offer a man a chance to work and to find new relationships, people who are just like you, but most slaves already lived on the land owned by the rich Romans. Their friendship is generally created around the other slaves who work for the same master. There are few opportunities to meet new friends bound the boundary of the land in which they serve.

How was Onesimus going to reach a citizen of Rome? Surely the landowner would ask him where he came from, and they would see who he really was by the way he dressed and the way he spoke. Thus, they would only offer him the same opportunities that he had in Colossae.

What the city would not offer a slave was an opportunity to elevate him. It's highly unlikely for him to become rich, famous, or to fall upon some rich Roman who would take him in, adopt him and place him into the high society of Rome. Yes, the big city appeared to be the answer to how he would change his life, just as the forbidden fruit seemed to be a blessing for Eve. As you know, once he arrived, reality set in, and Onesimus found himself in a strange city with his hope standing on shaky grounds.

Questions:

•What will it take to change your life? (Star Search, the X Factory, Dancing with the stars, big movie deal, the next promotion, marrying, hitting the lotto, losing weight, getting a face-lift.)

- What would be most important if you won the contest? Why?

- Would you see a life of helping others or controlling people?

- Discuss what you have tried with your group or with a friend.

Note:

Did you notice that the things you are hoping will change your future are things that fall into three categories: The lust of the eyes, the lust of the flesh, and the pride of life, which is 1 John 2:16

Jesus promised to supply our needs, not our wants. (25) Yet we should know by now that our needs are far more important than our wants. Until we become grateful for our needs, we cannot expect to receive our wants.

CHAPTER SEVEN

STEP OFF THE BUS

Do you believe that a change in location is what you need? Let me tell you, that the big city or a new city cannot change your life? Once you step off the bus, you will discover in your suitcase the same fears, the same low self-esteem, the same shortcomings that made you unsuccessful in the last city.

And some of you have become particularly good at pretending. We hide behind our masks, and we live in fear that someone will learn our ugly secret, and that is, we <u>are simply a slave who has run away</u>. We have merely become an expert in the game called pretense.

The secrets that you have hidden inside your suitcase are proof that change never took place. The old man is always lurking around, and only the power in the Word of God can shut down the old man.

You have a new spirit, but your soul is not regenerated. Thus, the old man old emotions, old way of thinking is yet there. Allow the power of God through the weapons He has given you; keep the old man under your feet. If you do not learn to control the flesh, every battle you are in, you will be defeated. The flesh will never stay out of the way, so put under and keep him there.

OLD MAN FLESH

We keep the old man, which is the flesh, under our feet. To keep him [old man] under, we must trust in the finished work of Christ Jesus. Because at the proper time, God extended His love towards us that while we were yet sinners, His Son, Jesus Christ, came and died for us. (26)

Before Jesus died, Gentiles were the ungodly. And we had no relationship with the Father because our sins stood between a holy God and us. Those who were Jewish, descendants of Abraham, had a ceremony where they used the blood of an animal to cover their sins. Still, the majority of the Gentiles were not a part of that ceremonial inheritance.

It was much later that the Gentiles became an engrafted branch. Until the appointed time, this engraftment was hidden from the people of Israel. God revealed it to his holy apostles and prophets. (27) This mystery revealed that the Gentiles would one day become heirs together with Israel. (28) Thus, making the Apostle Paul the church's overseer or Apostle over the Gentiles. Therefore, Christ died for us, the ungodly. (29) All sinful men needed a Savior.

We had little to no control over the things we said and did. Then Jesus came as the Son of Man and took our place upon the cross, and those who believe in Jesus Christ became new creatures in Christ. Old things passed away, and all things became new because of our new spirit. We are now connected, Spirit to spirit, with Jesus.

Who is in control in your temple? Will the old man continue to control you? Remember, he has only one concern, himself. Going from ordinary to extra-ordinary requires operating outside of the box. In this case, your box is your mindset. You can only be wiser when you are full of the Spirit. And the Spirit will not operate with the old selfish man.

David was a man after God's own heart, but when he became selfish and took another man's wife, he lost that anointing. The Spirit that rested upon kings in the Old Testament did not function again in David's life until he repented before God. God is merciful, He forgave David for killing Uriah and having an affair with Uriah's wife, but he [David] was punished for what he had done. The baby that Bathsheba was carrying died. War and bitterness raged through his family forever. Amnon rapes his sister, Tamar; Absalom kills Amnon and then turns against his father. David had to flee the city to save his life. When we do not keep the flesh under control, we will surely fall into sin. And that opens the door

47

to more corruption. Once that sin enters, your personality and lifestyle change for the worst. Maybe not so much in the eyes of some men, but in the eyes of God, who is Holly, you are rebellious.

When we review the word "rebellious," we find that in the Blue Letter Bible - Strong's definition describes rebellious as: mârâh, maw-raw'; a primitive root; to be (causatively, make) bitter (or unpleasant); (figuratively) to rebel (or resist; causatively, to provoke):—bitter, change, be disobedient, disobey, grievously, provocation, provoke(-ing), (be) rebel (against, -lious).

The old man/flesh will always be rebellious against the Word of God; therefore, how shall you please God that He may bless you and be with you if you are rebelling against His commands?

I warned you to change your destiny; it would require a fight. Keeping the old man under control is a fight you will have to face every day of your life. Be of good cheer, God is with you, and He is able to help you take control of the flesh and keep it under subjections.

Questions:

- Who are you? Do you have a spirit like King Saul, pretending to be great and full of confidence, but be careful that you do not find yourself fearful, doubtful, and full of jealousy? (Read: 1 Sam 18:9, 14, 15)

- Or are you like Judas Iscariot, pretending to be a disciple of Jesus. Yet, you wear a mask. (Read: Jhn 12:6)

- What type of rebellion has attached itself to your life?

Note:

Study more on the subject of being rebellious until you can identify your rebellious nature. The more you understand the impact of rebellion, the more it will help you stay in line. Nobody is perfect, for we all sin and fall short, but that is not an excuse not to try to do better. The more you trust God, the more you will be able to take back the areas of your life that the enemy has conquered. (Read: Deu 9:7, 24; Ezr. 4:15; Psa 78:8; Isa 1:23, 30:1, 9; 65:2)

CHAPTER EIGHT

CHANGE YOUR STARS

If you are going to change your life, you must change it before getting on the bus. At least begin the process of fixing things before buying the ticket. The ticket is an alternative method of resolving the issue. Running away never resolves the problem. If you try to fix the problem and then decide to leave, the new city can supply the next stage in your development. You must be intentional in changing your stars.

Reaching for the stars requires trusting in the plan of God. The more you love God, the better your chances of changing who you are. God will make the qualities in you better than before. Look at the life of any movie star or athlete. They have outstanding careers, but most have failed in their personal life. We see that beauty and talent do not guarantee you a Zoe life. The life that Jesus gives is greater than being a movie star, an athlete, a dancer, or even a singer. He has the power to make them better brothers, sisters, fathers, mothers, aunts, uncles, and neighbors. And some will become true heroes.

Without Christ in your life, you will never become the person that you dream of becoming. King Saul was anointed of God, but when he lost his anointing, he began to fail at everything. While King Saul was focused on capturing David and keeping his rights to the throne, he fell at being a godly man, a good father, and a great king.

While Judas Iscariot waited for Jesus to set up his kingdom over the Romans, he failed to be a devoted disciple of Christ. He could not see that Jesus was doing the will of his Father/God and not the wishes of man. Judas was selfish, he only thought of his desire, and that was to over-take the Romans. Thus, he became a thief as he stole from the money bag, and of course, he became a traitor when he betrayed Christ.

Therefore, the anointing of God is crucial in a person's life. Because it is His power that comes upon us that makes us a better person, thus we are able in Christ to think differently, act differently, and talk differently. That is because God is on the inside of us, leading us and teaching us how to be holy men and women of God.

Therefore, changing your stars and breaking out of a mundane life is accepting the Zoe life Christ offers to every person who will believe in God and the finished work of Christ.

JESUS

Jesus was the son of Mary and Joseph, The Savior of the World, the Son of God, the mentor of twelve disciples, a friend to the believers, a teacher, the Truth, and the Light. He is the good shepherd and the Bright and Morning Star. He is the 'I AM.' He was more than a prophet, more than a priest, more than a son; he was God in the flesh, the Messiah.

He came so that he could change our lives. He came to fulfill the law and bridge the gap between God and man. Jesus did not change his destiny, but he fulfilled it. This atonement was required so that you could change your destiny. Now a man can stop his negative thinking. You are no longer poor in thought and pitiful in action.

Hope is now strong, and life has new meaning. You have become a Christian who now has rights and privileges that come from heaven. And when Jesus finished making a way for us to have a better life in God, He became our high priest, and He sent the Holy Spirit to dwell within us, to lead us and guide us.

Once you accept Jesus as your Lord and Savior, nothing will ever be the same unless you choose to revert to the pig pen of life you once had. Jesus said if He abides in you, you can ask what you will, and He will do it. (30)

He told you whatever ye shall ask of the Father in the name of Jesus; you can expect to receive from God. (31) Do you see having a new mindset gives you access to the Father. Why would you not accept such a gracious offer? The Father is

52

offering you a chance to be exceptional, and all you have to do is let Him into your life.

Here is the/your break you have been hoping for. Now the God of the universe is offering to meet your needs so you can become the person you know you are capable of being. For sure, you shall receive if you ask in faith if you do not waver. (32) We cannot operate in faith and doubt at the same time. You must take a stand as to which side you are going to stand on. But consider this: little faith, little power. God does not get involved unless there is faith involved. You must believe that He exists and that He is capable of meeting your needs.

We must learn to balance our lives even if it takes a lifetime to do, but as we receive our helper (Holy Spirit), we will conquer more areas of our lives. You will be full of joy that surpasses happiness. And maybe you will find peace where you were before, and there will be no need to buy a bus ticket to the big city. The decision is yours.

Questions:

- When will you ask God to help you? (Read: James 1:5)
- Have you asked Jesus about receiving the abundant life He offers? (Read: Luk 1:37)
- What's hindering your belief? (Read: Prov 11:2)

CHAPTER NINE

BIG CITY - ROME

When Onesimus reached Rome, imagine him roaming the streets, watching the sights, and enjoying the sounds that echo within the city itself. These sights and sounds indicate it was a thriving city.

Onesimus made sure he kept his distance from the Roman soldiers and those who would lead him into trouble. The excitement and smell of this great city almost overwhelmed him. He was glad he ran away. By now, he had traded in the item he stole as soon as he arrived, and it gave him the freedom to roam and enjoy all the finer things that Rome could offer, at least for a couple of days.

Onesimus' story is like unto the prodigal son. Both men were trying to escape their past. One ran away, and the other walked away. They both got as far as possible and all for the same reasons. They ran because they believed life was better somewhere else. Until the money ran out and they fell on hard times did they began to think of home. They probably debated what they should have done or could have done if they had been wiser with their spending.

The prodigal son sold himself into servitude to a pig farmer, and Onesimus thought about selling himself to someone he felt he could rely upon, but he did not know anyone in Rome. When both men had suffered enough, the prodigal son rose up and recognized that he had sinned.

He returned home with a humble heart and a willingness to be a servant to his earthly father. He could surrender to his earthly father because he had turned himself over to his heavenly Father through repenting. Onesimus eventually repented, and he did return home with the same spirit of the prodigal son.

Repentance will always restore one with the Father. If he had not set things right with God, he would never have had the courage to return home with such a meek and humble spirit. Onesimus repented to the Father and received Jesus as his Lord and Savior. It was much later, but he eventually returned to the servitude of his master, Philemon. But I have given you the ending, yet we must continue to examine how he came to repent.

Before there is a submissive spirit, there is a rebellious one. Our bad decisions are always catching up to us. History generally repeats itself when we do not learn that God will not bless a contrary person. He allows our past to collide with our present to get our attention. When that disaster happens, we find ourselves standing in a bigger mess than before.

MONEY GONE

Like all good things must come to an end, and thus, the money runs out reality returns. How shall Onesimus survive without money? He is not in Colossae, where Philemon supplied food and shelter. Now the two men [prodigal son and a slave] are once again miserable and lost. Hard times bring about truth. Our once blinded eyes can now see what truth is. And the ability to see clear somehow removes the fog that clouded our judgment.

The decision to run away and find happiness somewhere else proved to be more challenging than originally expected. And all the newfound friends are nowhere to be found. Neither the prodigal son nor Onesimus had prepared themselves for tomorrow's troubles. The enemy seems to blind us when he tricks us. Or do we become blind by the thing that tempts us? However, our blindness comes; it causes us to see only one thing, the object we desire.

It is our forbidden fruit that causes us to distort reality. I am sure that Onesimus fantasized about all the good things that would happen for him in the big city. As long as there is money to burn,

56

the fantasy will continue. But one day, the money did run out, and the dream ended.

Just as Eve admired the fruit from afar, her possibilities of what it would taste like were endless. One day she decided to stop imagining, and she tasted the forbidden fruit, and when she did, she woke up in a nightmare. The price for tasting the fruit was far more terrifying than she was aware.

See her standing outside the Garden of Eden, knowing that she cannot go back in and fellowship with the Father. She can yet see the beautiful things that the garden possesses, but she cannot touch them.

I suppose Onesimus thought about going back home for a moment. He remembered Philemon's land and the things he had to do as a slave there. There were no happy memories for him, thus returning home was not an option.

What can Onesimus do? He is just another slave wandering in the city of Rome. It is estimated that there were about 300,000 to 350 000 slaves in Rome around the first century AD. (33) And just as you conceived, there was no tolerance for another poor slave in Roman. Who was going to lend a hand towards a way ward slave?

PERSECUTION

With so many people in slavery, where would Onesimus find food and shelter? If he went to any rich Roman citizen, he would only become another slave with a new master to please. And without money, who would support him? Sometimes reality is a hard pill to swallow.

BREAKING OR MAKING

It is quoted by many that persecution will either make you or break you. I say <u>when persecution comes</u>, it can do both. It will hurt you, as I am sure it did Onesimus. Onesimus woke up one morning and realized he had nothing. This feeling made him appear useless again. He was cast into the streets with the other run-away slaves and thieves.

How long could Onesimus remain in Rome without food or money before he would be forced to join the thieves in the city? After a couple of days without food, I am sure Onesimus would have resorted to a life of crime or servitude to stay alive.

Persecution can also make you into a better person. In Onesimus' case, persecution made him. At the time Onesimus was in Rome, the Apostle Paul was there under house arrest.

Otherwise, the Apostle Paul would not have been available for Onesimus to meet. (34)

It is more reasonable to assume that God led this poor slave to a Christian servant. Or do you think He led the Christian slave to Onesimus?

This compassionate brother took Onesimus in and fed him and told him about Jesus and His Apostles. With Onesimus lacking in all areas of his life, he had no choice but to eat what was served and listen to what was being said.

Your character either has the will to fight or the will to lose. Onesimus chose to fight. And out of his newfound quality in his character, Onesimus discover there is hope in Christ Jesus. (35) Did Onesimus have character? Yes, he did. His mental and ethical traits told him that he could be more than a slave. It gave him the desire to want more than what he had; thus, the decision to run away was due to his strong character.

For we know had he not run away, he might not have found what he really needed, Jesus Christ. But a strong character must have a humble spirit before the Lord. (36) I believed Onesimus cried out to the God of his understanding, and The God of heaven and earth responded to him. God allows pressure to be applied to our lives to cause us to surrender to His will. Therefore, difficulties will break you and then make you into a better person.

Questions:

- Who or what woke you up after biting your forbidden fruit? (Read: Matt 15:14)

- Can you recover from a bad decision? (Read: Acts 2:38)

- Why is it important to make choices with help from God? (Read: 2 Cho. 20:9;Ps 121:2)

CHAPTER TEN

GOD'S PLAN

What happens when God calls you out or answers your call? From the moment He turns towards you, you can cry out hallelujah. The abundant life begins moving towards you, and you are not even fully aware of what is about to happen.

God placed His hand upon Onesimus a long time ago. We know this because we see how the evidence. He...God watched over Onesimus as he traveled to Rome. He cared for him as he wandered through the streets. He enjoyed the sights of the city as he sought a safe place of rest.

It was God who kept the Roman soldiers from capturing him and throwing him into prison, which is what the soldiers would have done to any runaway slave. He would have been confined until Philemon came to claim him. He protected him from those who would have taken advantage of Onesimus.

Onesimus was not aware, but God was in control. God is an expert in guiding one down the right path. For God knows that applied pressure will produce the results, He wants from us.

And when we realized that our plan did not work the way we thought it would, and our backs were against the wall, we cried out to Him. It is the same type of urgent cry that the Israelites did in Egypt when they were slaves. And they also cried out to God when being carried away by the Babylonian king Nebuchadnezzar.

WHEN WE CRY OUT

It is the crying of God's children that draws Him unto us. That is why I believe that Onesimus cried out to God, and He responded. Our cry for help opens the door or invites God into our dilemma. He wants us to depend upon Him. And when we do, He takes care of us like a mother with a newborn baby. He guides us like a Father would when a toddler is taking their first steps.

The Word of God tells us that God loved us first. (37) When we did not love ourselves, love was reaching out towards us. We were God's elect, chosen before the foundation of the world to be holy and blameless before Him. (38) The bible tells us that it pleased the Father to predestine us through adoption. From adoption, we become children by Jesus Christ. (39) We see that

Onesimus was one of those predestined children of God. The Apostle Paul learned that he too was a predestined child of God even though he had aided in capturing and murdering Christians.

He discovered it on the road of Damascus. The once independent Paul found himself blinded by the light of Jesus. He became spiritually alive and physically blind.

The great Paul, the defender of everything sacred to the Jews, was now being led helplessly by others. He turned towards God through prayer and fasting. His divine appointment with Christ on the road and his blindness caused Paul to surrender to the will of God.

There on Straight Street, he waited upon the Lord, and thus, God sent a prophet named Ananias to pray for him and open his blinded eyes. (40)Now it was Onesimus' turn to cry out to God for help. And in so crying out, I believe God sent a servant of His to Onesimus. The servant of the Lord took him home and fed him. As they fellowshipped, the servant of the Lord spoke of Christ, his burial, and resurrection. And as all Christians do, he invited Onesimus to go to the Apostle Pauls' house.

HOUSEBOUND

Now let us fast forward to the present again. The Apostle is housebound. If he were not a prisoner in his own home, the Apostle would not have been available. Paul would probably be traveling from city to city preaching and instructing the churches. But God made sure the Apostle was in one specific place that he might minister to Onesimus. Yes, the same Apostle who once had his own eyes opened to the truth is now assigned to open Onesimus.

AFTER THE HOLY GHOST

The life of a slave was limited. He could not walk off the master's land or sit under a shaded tree and read the latest novel or self-help book that would change his destiny. We are not sure if Onesimus could read or write, and we are not sure how well he could articulate his words. But I tell you, after the Holy Ghost comes upon a man/woman, they who were once illiterate will begin to speak eloquently.

They will have the wisdom to profound the wise. When the Holy Ghost comes upon a repenting soul, one can do far more than the original man could.

THE DISCIPLES

Look at the disciples of Jesus, twelve men who were unlearned and uneducated—chosen to demonstrate the love and power of God. They taught the world about Jesus, God's perfect sacrifice. But these things did not come about by their natural talent or gifts. When the Holy Spirit came into the upper room, He transformed their lives. They did not have to develop or buy or go to school to preach the Gospel.

Everything was inside them the moment the Spirit sat upon each one of them. They spoke in tongues as proof that the Holy Spirit had come to dwell inside them. With their new spirit connecting with Christ through the Holy Spirit, the power of God was able to work in them and by them.

See, the power of the Holy Spirit goes beyond the normal; it takes a believer into the Spirit realm where supernatural things of God await them. Those supernatural things are brought forth through prayer or decrees. It is the Spirit of God that takes your spoken word into the spiritual realm.

The words that are spoken have authorization and power because what was said included faith in God, a promise of God, and the name of Jesus. This type of prayer gives the believer the right to make the request. The prayer enters into the supernatural and brings back what it needs for a specific issue. How else could men and women of Jesus be able to travel and preach the good news?

When the disciples walked with Christ for three and a half years, they had little power. The power that was working was the power that lived in Christ. But when the Holy Spirit came upon them, after the death and resurrection of Christ. They found they had the same authority to do as Christ did. Miracles, signs, and wonders followed them just as Jesus told them it would. Did he not say to them?

"Behold, I give unto you power to tread on serpents and scorpions, and overall, the power of the enemy: and nothing shall by any means hurt you." (41)

And did he not tell his seventy [70] disciples that he sent out, not to be joyful that evil spirits obeyed them. But they should be glad that their names were written in the book of life. (42) Therefore, their power came from on high and not by their own making.

Not only were the disciples able to heal and deliver the sick, but the Holy Spirit had begun to produce the fruit of the Spirit in their lives. They even spoke in tongues, prophesied, resisted snake bits, and endured imprisonment. It was customary to receive a beating for speaking the name of Jesus. They all lost their lives for the sake of Christ so that Onesimus would find his life in Christ.

We, too, can be grateful that the first group of disciples prevailed against the darkness of this world. Now others may hear about Jesus who died for their sins. And we today are blessed by their efforts as well.

Patience teaches us that there is joy in our testing because the Spirit is developing us. (43) Tests come to empower our faith to grow stronger in the Lord. Expected suffering and joy is the type of cross we must bear. Yet, there are periods of resting after a testing experience. There are times when we must pull back from the front line of the battle to come and rest. It allows us to be re-energized for the next round. This resting is a time of refreshing. Sometimes while resting, the urgency we once felt passes, and peace reigns again in our hearts. We also find we have the strength to endure or the courage to overcome that difficult trial.

Let us look at the Corina Virus as our example. When the virus showed up, the entire world was in turmoil. This was a major crisis that the whole world had to face together. Then God had mercy upon us, and He gave knowledge to man to create a vaccine. Although the virus is yet with us, the urgency is not as great as it once appeared.

Each critical moment draws us closer to God. It causes us to see how vulnerable we are and how much we need God in our lives. And those who take on the challenges of this world alone will lead themselves into deeper trouble. They found substitutes to bring them peace. They use drugs and alcohol as an antidote. They spend all their time making money to find satisfaction or to give them power. These are temporary fixes that do not resolve the deeper issue. Only in Christ shall one find real peace that lasts.

And if we must wait for the full effect of our change to come, we find that we are yet transforming into the image of Christ. Our minds and our conduct are being replaced with a new mindset and with new behavior. In time we learn what not to do in a situation by what we experienced in our past. "So, let patience have its perfect work." (44)

When you look at the life of Peter, we see He started with a rough edge, but as he walked with Jesus for three-plus years, he learned the value of patience. He learned to speak slowly, be slow to anger, and be quick to hear. (45)

Questions:

• Where in your life has patience had its perfect work in you? (Read: James 1:4)

- Have you experienced persecution
  For the sake of Christ, and if so,
  what did you learn from it?
  (Read: Acts 13:50, 11:13; Rom
  8:35; 2 Tim 3:12)

- Does standing still appears to be
  impossible for you in a time of
  turmoil? (Read: Exo 14:13; 2 Cho
  20:17)

CHAPTER ELEVEN

HOPE

When it is all said and done, hope springs forth, and what was once a dark day is replaced with sunshine. Hope is the expectation of something good before the change has fully taken place. (46) It is also the expectation of something good before it ever manifests.

Hope births faith, and faith is the substance of what we are hoping to receive from God. Our faith is the evidence of things not seen. (47) Therefore, we have faith that what we prayed for will happen because we prayed to our Father God in the name of Jesus, and we prayed in faith—believing that God would answer our request. That is truly a promise from Jesus. (48)

As Onesimus walked the streets unwanted, unloved, and without a friend, God moved again in his direction. Onesimus did not have the kind of friends that Job had. When Job's body was covered with sores, his friends came and sat on the ground with him for seven days and nights, never speaking a word. (49) The physical presence of his friends was his support.

Rest assured that when you have Jesus, you have more than enough. He will have a stranger, or He will send an enemy to your rescue. (50) God sent an angel to unlock the prison doors for the Apostle Peter as the people prayed for his release. Another example is the riot in Ephesus, where the people were stirred up against the disciples because they thought they had to protect their way of worshipping.

Demetrius, the silversmith, was the real instigator of the riot. He did not care about the goddess Artemis but the loss of his livelihood. The crowd took the disciples and dragged them into the arena, and they shouted the name of the goddess Artemis for two hours. It took the city clerk to calm the people down. Then they all left the arena, which freed the disciples of God. (51)

Whoever it was that came to Onesimus rescue brought hope back into his life. And from there, the divine appointment clock began to whine down until he met the Apostle Paul and received salvation.

What saved Onesimus is that he was willing to open his heart like the Ethiopian, the overseer for the treasury of Kandake, queen of the Ethiopians.

The Ethiopian was reading the book of Isaiah. He was confused, for he did not understand what he had read. Then the Holy Spirit instructed Philip to join himself to the Ethiopian chariot. After he expounded on the book of Isaiah, the Ethiopian understood and received the Word of

God. Thus, he asked to be baptized as the Word indicated. (52)

Can you visualize how this Christian was called to show kindness to Onesimus? First, he offered his friendship and willingness to help him. He may have said to him, "Does thou need help, my friend." Or maybe he was more direct and told him, "God has instructed me to help you."

Whatever he said and however he approached Onesimus, he made the connection. After fulfilling his physical need, it was time to meet his spiritual one.

Somewhere in their conversation, he told Onesimus about Jesus and His disciples. Then he said that one of His disciples was living right here in Rome. An invitation was given to go to the Apostle Paul's house, and Onesimus accepted. Onesimus believed what he heard, and he received salvation that day in the Apostle's home.

THE MESSAGE

Here is what he might have heard: "Do not be selfish nor try to impress others but humble yourselves by putting the other man's needs first. (53) Take an interest in your neighbor. (54) This is the right attitude that Christ commands of us. (55)

Even though Jesus was the Son of God, He did not hold on to that title. (56) But He gave up that holy title and exalted position to become a humble servant and a human being. (57) Once a man, Jesus became obedient to God, and he fulfilled his mission. He died between two criminals on the cross. (58) He died for the entire world so that every man could be reconciled to God.

Each man must choose to receive Christ as their Savior or to reject Him. He must believe in the life, death, burial, and resurrection of Jesus. And one day, every tongue shall confess that Jesus Christ is Lord. (59) Jesus Christ offers you a new life, a new beginning, and a home in heaven. Oh, how Onesimus could identify with Jesus coming into the world as a servant, a lowly person. He felt his hope rising as he heard that Jesus came to save the world, to give everyone a second chance.

Onesimus desired a second chance, and he wanted that new life in Christ Jesus. This was the reason he ran away from Colossae. It was then that he forgot about everything that frustrated him. He surrenders himself to the power of God and his Savior, Christ Jesus.

THE CHANGE

From that moment, Onesimus felt that a change had taken place. He wanted to know more about

Jesus. He returned to the Apostle Paul's house every day feasting on The Word of God. The two men bonded quickly in the spirit.

Onesimus was thirsty for the Word, just as the Ethiopian whom Philip helped. (60) Remember, he yearned to be baptized after the scriptures were explained to him. (61)The Word became alive in his soul. His demeanor changed. Truly the old man was dethroned. With his new spirit, he served God by serving the Apostle Paul.

Being a servant was no longer offensive to him. There is a difference between wanting to serve and being forced to act. The volunteer way comes from the peace and joy one receives by receiving Jesus as Lord and Savior. Believers obey to give glory to God. Your blessing extends beyond mere happiness. You find joy in serving unto God, who is also a rewarder to all who will obey Him.

To be forced to serve is controlling a person's bodily action without controlling the necessary will of that person. You may get them to do what you demand, but when you are not there, they will put little effort into the task that is being asked of them.

Many supervisors have learned that in order to get people to work hard for them, the people must feel respected and believe that they have a relationship/connection with the supervisor.

Onesimus felt he had a relationship with the Apostle Paul. And as he learned about God and what He expected out of Onesimus, he worked hard serving the apostle. He wanted his life to count for something. He wanted to give God the glory as he served Paul and the Christian community in Rome.

SONSHIP

Then the time came when the Apostle Paul had to share another truth about his relationship with the Father. He told Onesimus that a slave does not have a place in the family of God. Therefore, he must stop seeing himself as one. <u>He is now a son of God,</u> who is now a part of The Body of Christ. (62) When going from ordinary to extraordinary, one must learn to see themselves as the new creature one has become. Being a new creature entitles you to be called a son or a child of God.

Paul taught how slaves are to act toward their master. He told them not to allow the fact that they are someone's property trouble them. If they can gain their freedom, do so. (63) Onesimus realized that it was okay to want to be free, and if God sets him free, then he shall be free, but if not, he can yet live an abundant life in Christ.

He learned that there are no Jews, Gentiles, males, or females in The Body of Christ. Then the Apostle told him that there are no slaves nor servants nor bond maidens in Christ either. (64) Everyone is free in the Body of Christ, and everyone is equal, leaving Christ as the head. Because Christ is the head of the church, and we are "sons of God," we can no longer be segregated into groups such as: circumcised, uncircumcised, barbaric, or uncivilized.

If a believer must have a label, then let them be referred to as Christians, followers of Christ. Christ is the only thing that matters. (65)

His love for God grew because he could see that God truly did understand his desire to be free and his zeal to become a better person. As Onesimus visited the Apostle Paul, he instructed Onesimus how to serve his master. It must be, he said, " with a single heart." If one does well, as you do your job, Christ will reward you. (66) He was glad also to know that even his master, Philemon, must serve with a sincere heart. For now, Onesimus knows that God is not a respecter of persons. (67)

RETURNING HOME

As Onesimus was allowing the Word of God to tell him who he was, it was also telling him what he must do to set things right. As he stood before the Apostle, he was convicted in his spirit that returning home was the right solution. He was no longer afraid, for he had found what he had been looking for all his life. Thus, he was secure that whatever decision God had made for him would be just and fair. The rest he would leave in the hands of Philemon.

Thus, the Apostle wrote a letter to Philemon to influence his thinking. Onesimus could see that he had a true friend indeed because his friend was willing to write to Philemon to help settle the matter between him and his master.

PAUL'S STRATEGY

I can understand how difficult it was for the Apostle Paul to tell Onesimus that it was time for him to return home to Colossae. I know that both of their hearts were broken even though they knew they were making the right decision. Paul's strategy was to write a good explanation by hand in hopes that Philemon would read his letter before responding to the presence of Onesimus.

The Apostle Paul wanted his co-worker [Philemon] to see that running away was to escape the mundane life he had. He needed to explain that there was a purpose in the running…God was at the helm of this entire matter. What started as a selfish act, an act of rebellion, has turned into a triple blessing. Onesimus was born again, the Apostle Paul was given another son, and Philemon has a quality servant and brother in the faith.

Questions:

- If you were to open your suitcase, what would you find hidden among the relics of your mind? (Read: Rom 3:2)

- Would you agree with the Apostle Paul that it was right for Onesimus to return home? (Read: Psa 37:37, 125:4; Luk 2:29; 2 Tim 4:6-8; Isa 32:17)

- What type of attitude did you have when you returned to face the error of your actions? (Read: Heb1:3; Hos 8:13; Deu 29:29; Num 5:1)

PART TWO

THE LETER

The lesson covers: Phm 1:1-3

Paul, a prisoner of Christ Jesus, and Timothy our brother, To Philemon our dear friend and fellow worker— (Phm 1:1)

also, to Apphia, our sister, and Archippus, our fellow soldier--and to the church that meets in your home: (Phm 1:2)

Grace and peace to you from God our Father and the Lord Jesus Christ. (Phm 1:3)

DISCUSSION:

Paul begins to write a letter to Philemon. He has a few important things to tell him, but how shall he begin? It appears that he decided to start his letter with his normal greeting. Yet, in this particular letter to Philemon, he decides to include two specific people that have a close associa-tion with Philemon. Is this being clever, or does he write with no underlining intentions?

My story version of verses: 1-3:

"As the Apostle sat at his table at midnight seeking God for His directions and guidance, the Holy Spirit falls upon him as he begins his letter to Philemon:

Greetings to you, my dear friend and fellow worker in the Lord; Timothy asks me to say hello as well since we are all prisoners of Christ Jesus. I cannot offer enough praises to you, my friend, because of all the hard work you have done for the Lord. Anyone who is as devoted as you, Philemon, I consider a fellow worker. For you, take your assignment seriously, and it reflects in what you have already carried out in Colossae."

Let me stop right here and acknowledge your wife, Apphia, for I hear that she proves to have the same work efforts as you. And let us not overlook your son, Archippus, who is also a fellow soldier." "How are the people who attend your services? Please let them know that I send salutation to them because they continue to show themselves faithful to the church. May God bless them for their desire to hear the Word. If I have overlooked anyone, Philemon, please tell them not to count it against me. I want to greet everyone in your family and those who labor faithfully in God's house because every believer has a place in my heart, especially the dedicated ones."

"I truly want that the grace and peace of our Father God continue to rest upon each one of you. For the Lord's kindness is what we receive when we sacrifice all for The Kingdom of God. It is an honor to salute all my brothers and sisters."

DISCUSSION:

Immediately we see, the Apostle names the leaders that operate at the church in Colossae, thus giving specific honorable mention to Philemon, who serves at that church. The letter was designed to also appeal to him because the Apostle addresses Philemon's wife, Apphia, and possible son, Archippus. (68)

Some theologians claim Archippus as the bishop or possibly the church pastor in Colossae, and some believed him to be Philemon's son or a family member. (69)

If Archippus was his son, then he is flattering Philemon even more by taking the time to include him in the letter. He not only mentions him, but he refers to him as a "fellow soldier." This surely would impress Philemon's entire family that the great Apostle Paul has included this young man in the struggle of life.

It surely tells us that Archippus is not a lazy man. It identifies him as a brave and honorable Christian who is not ashamed of the gospel of Jesus Christ. The Apostle greets this young man as he has done to other courageous men in his earlier letters. He did it in Philippians 2:25 with Epaphroditus, and in 2 Timothy, he acknowledges Timothy, and in Colossians 4:47-18, he speaks again of Archippus.

This letter will be read in a church service, and when it does, everyone will hear and know that the Apostle Paul has high regard for Archippus. With sincerity, the Apostles continue to give respect to Philemon by referring to him as a friend and fellow worker. Once he includes his entire family, he can rest assured that he has Philemon's interest.

Yet, the Apostle dives deeper into Philemon's heart by making him aware that he knows the sacrifices he is making for the church at Colossae. Not only is he aware, but he is acknowledging that the church in Colossae is in existence and functioning because of Philemon's love for God's people.

There isn't anyone who does not appreciate when their efforts are recognized. Therefore, I say that this was a brilliant strategy on the part of the Apostle Paul to begin his letter in a way that includes all the good things he knows that Philemon and his family were doing.

Yet, I believe this letter was hard for the Apostle to write because he had to explain two very important things. First, he must explain that he knows where Onesimus is, and secondly, he must tell Philemon that his slave has been working for him all this time in Rome.

Can a person properly explain in written words that they are sorry? Will Paul be able to truly express to Philemon that he understands and regrets the strain he put him through? Paul knew that he should have shared the secret long before now. It would have relieved Philemon of his concern for his slave.

How do you say that with pen and ink? Will Philemon feel a deep sorrow that the Apostle is experiencing? Paul will not be able to hear Philemon read the letter. He will not hear his responses nor see his facial expressions, which would signify that he had expressed his sorrow correctly. So, he writes to Philemon and sends the letter off with a prayer that everything he said would be accurate and filled with the expectation that all is forgiven.

Questions:

- If you had to explain a hidden secret, how did you [or would you] present it to your friend family member? (Read Psa 19:12, 69:5, 38:9,139:15; Ecc. 12:14)

- How would you have addressed Philemon if he was your friend? (Read: Matt 23:12,7: 12,18:21; Eph 4:2; 1 Pe 3:8

STAGE TWO

This lesson covers: Phm 1:4-7

> I always thank my God as I re-
> member   you in my prayers,
> (Phm 1:4)

> because I hear about your love for
> all his holy people and your faith
> in the Lord Jesus. (Phm 1:5)

> I pray that your partnership with us
> in the faith may be effective in
> deepening your understanding of
> every good thing we share for the
> sake of Christ.   (Phm 1:6)

> Your love has given me great joy
> and encouragement because you,
> brother, have refreshed the hearts
> of the Lord's people.   (Phm 1:7)

DISCUSSION:

Can a letter truly express the heart of a person?
Does it take a special writer to explain to a
friend what happened, or can this writer [Paul]

truly explain the reason they are making such a request? The Apostle Paul is trying to tell his friend through paper and pin about love, forgiveness, and an opportunity to gain experience in the Lord. May he be successful in fulfilling his task?

My story version of verses: 4-7

"Did you know that I always pray to God for you, Philemon, and the church in your home? I pray because I see the unselfish sacrifices that you continually make for the church. You could be taking that time and giving it to your family or managing your home and business. I can imagine there are several chores required to keep things in balance at home. Yet, despite all the things that I imagine you do, you take the time to run the church and meet the needs of those who attend."

"I pray most earnestly for you because I know the burden that these sacrifices can put on a man-of-god who is trying to oversee his people. And I see that despite the responsibility, the love in your heart keeps extending outwardly. It excites me to see such a fellow worker labor the way you do. Your labor is an act of love. I have heard of your efforts. Therefore, I know that it is Christ's love that keeps you going. It is that same love that saved you and began you on your journey."

"You are truly a blessing to have as a partner. If I partner with anyone, may it always be with those who love and care for God's holy people? May they be willing to share what they have in order that The Body of Christ is **filled, full, and satisfied**? And they are satisfied in Colossae, Philemon." "I also pray that your faith increases as you labor for the Lord. And that each level will deepen your experience through the Holy Spirit. An Active Life in the Holy Spirit produces more good works. Philemon, this is what we share as brothers in Christ, Philemon."

"We have the Holy Spirit, and He assigns each of us our place in the Body. We are the mouth of Christ because we are called to share the gospel. You labor with intentions in Colossae and me, wherever the Holy Spirit leads me." "Have you come to realize that we are doing the same work for the Lord? May each day your spirit becomes more and more enlightened about what your responsibilities are and how important those obligations affect the Kingdom of God."

"May each step you take for the Lord cause His light to spread in the city of Colossae. But more than that, may your consciousness understand what, why, and when that is asked of you. And may you always answer the call with a YES."

DISCUSSION:

Again, in these four verses, The Apostle flatters him by telling him that he has him on his prayer list. And the reason he is on his top ten list is due to his faithfulness to the work of the Lord's Kingdom. The Apostle sees the need in Colosse, and Philemon has the power to complete the work.

Philemon's job is so important that the Apostle tells him that a great blessing is coming with such responsibilities. His blessing is a deeper love for God and a greater insight into the work that is needed in that city.

The Apostle believes that Philemon understands that his work is important and that he is making a difference. He also knows that Philemon is determined to complete it. Therefore, he reminds him that his efforts are not in vain; there are multiple blessings for him on earth and in heaven.

Again, he reminds him that they share the same goal, the same purpose, the same cross, and that is for the Lord Jesus Christ. Oh, how the compliments are flowing from the Apostle's heart to Philemon. Philemon might question if he is equal in strength/task to the Apostle Paul.

Yet, it flatters him to know that the apostle proclaims that they have the same value and work ethic. And that they have the same level of importance in sharing the gospel for The Kingdom. And finally, Philemon becomes aware that all of his efforts bring joy to the Apostle's heart.

The purpose of this letter is to touch Philemon's heart while it is setting things in place to inform him of Onesimus' whereabouts. He wants Philemon to know the "how" and "why" they have such a great relationship. The how involves the fact that they have the same heart. The reason why they have this relationship is that they have Christ in their lives. The love of Christ is motiving them to share the gospel. If the Apostle is clear enough, then Philemon will understand why he kept Onesimus so long. He is trying to explain that it was not a selfish reason but for the sake of the gospel.

I ask you; do you think Philemon has a little bit of pride in him, which is why Paul is flattering him so much? Tell me, do you think he is trying to boost his pride? Oh, do not think he does not have any? Every man has a little left-over pride that needs to be removed. And this pride that we have can be touched through sweet talk.

Or I say that it is Paul's wisdom that saturates the letter? He wishes to compliment Philemon to the highest level because he has earned it. Therefore, this is a good type of flattery that can be mentioned every now and then.

There are two old sayings that work when one has to share difficult news:

- ❖ You catch more flies with honey than with vinegar.
- ❖ You get more bees with honey.

The Apostle is trying to woo Philemon over to his side before he enlightens him about his missing property. And what better way than to start your conversation with as many accolades as possible.

If one is going to ask another for a great favor, it would be highly recommended to expound on the good things that the person has done or on the good things they have done for you. The harder Philemon works in Colossae, the less trouble the Apostle will have to deal with writing additional letters. Remember Jesus called the Apostle Paul to reach the Gentiles and to oversee the churches that he set up.

When the Apostle can choose a good leader to stay and run a church, that makes his burden lighter. It was an honor for Philemon to find out how the Apostle Paul felt about him. He would be more impressed to hear that his service for the Lord's people had made its way to Rome.

Questions:

- What would you do to woo your friend when you know that there is more to the story than they may be ready to hear? (Read: Eph 4:25-3:2l; Zec 8:16b; Prov 12:17, 17, Psa 15:2; Gal 4:16)

- How far will you go to get what you need? (Read: Exo 32:26-27; Matt 27: 17-26)

- There is a balance to manipulation before it turns sour. (Read: 1 Sam 15: 23; Lev 25:17;1 Thess. 4:6; Lev 19:11)

- Is there a good side and a bad side to manipulation? (Read: 1 Sam 15:22; Prov 125:5, 2:5; Isa 59:8)

STAGE THREE

This lesson covers: Phm 1:8-10 NIV

> Therefore, although in Christ I could be bold and order you to do what you ought to do, (Phm 1:8)

> yet I prefer to appeal to you on the basis of love. It is as none other than Paul--an old man and now also a prisoner of Christ Jesus - (Phm 1:9)

> that I appeal to you for my son Onesimus, who became my son while
> I was in chains. (Phm 1:10)

DISCUSSION

The letter goes on to the possibility of flexing muscles, meaning the Apostle Paul could demand from Philemon, but love is greater. There was a time, the Apostle would have flexed his muscles and used his authority to have his way, but now he is old and much wiser, and he knows now that he must do all things in love.

Just as he loves Onesimus as a son and would possibly do anything to save him, it does not give him the right to use his authority as a weapon. There is a time when the leader's authority is necessary, and there are times when authority can be abusive. God asks us to walk with Him in complete faith because He is the only one that will not abuse His authority.

The Apostle recognized that he had the wrong thought concerning the matter of Onesimus, and now the Apostle Paul turns to another more excellent way of making a point.

This lesson covers: Phm 1:8

> Therefore, although in Christ I could be
> bold and order you to do what you ought
> to do, (Phm 1:18)

DISCUSSION:

We see that Paul finds the right answer on how to manage this issue, but he wants Philemon to see his heart even though his heart reveals a negative thought. He corrects that negative thought by casting down the imagination that tries to exhaust itself above Christ. The Apostle is determined that the right way to approach this is with tender loving care.

My story version of verse: 1:8

Paul thinks within himself and thus writes: "I could be bold and order you to do what you ought to do." (70) But I am unction by a Spirit greater than I. This sweet Spirit which comes from heaven, whispers to me softly, "Do you really want to use your authority carelessly?" "What is greater, to use your authority to get your way or to humble yourself with humility and ask in love?"

"Flexing one's muscles is not always the best answer or the safest solution to a problem. You must first decide how important it is to have your way. Or are you willing to cross unnecessary boundaries to get what you want versus coming to another believer with an open heart and the spirit of gentleness?"

"And I imagine the Apostle responding to the Spirit, saying: "Thank you, Holy Spirit, for preventing me from using my authority in a situation that could be managed with humility."

Then the Apostle begins to write again, and he confronts the enemy who is tempting him: "I will not use my authority to get what I want from Philemon. For my heart has been checked by the Holy Spirit. I see the path I was about to go down, and it is what I want to do, but it is not what I must do. God is in control of everything, and I am being reminded that if I turn all things over to Him, the right solution will always follow." Because in my own power, I would fail.

"The thing I want to do, I find myself not doing, but the things I don't want to do is what I find myself doing, but thanks be-to-God, He has given me the Holy Spirit to dwell within me. The Spirit of correction, the Spirit of peace, the one I must always submit to, is setting my spirit on the right path. I can now see that the path of flesh would not serve me well in this case. I will not set myself above another concerning any issue, for to do so is to misuse my authority/power."

"I can feel the old man rising up in my thoughts. But I say gentleness is the choice I will make. The Holy Spirit will help me as I tell him that I am not above him in any way when it concerns this matter, for I am not blind concerning what is rightfully his.

I recognize that the authority that rests upon me has been given to me to build The Kingdom and not my selfishness." "For now, I see, if I were to demand my way, I would also lose my way. Selfishness will destroy the peace and the unity that dwells among brothers and sisters in Christ. He, whom I consider as my son, is also another man's property.

Which is fairer, to fight to save my son in the Lord or to acknowledge my brother's rights over my own? "I find that it is wiser to ask a favor from my brother with a glad heart than to apply un-godly pressure on him in order to win. Only God knows what is best for Onesimus. And I must trust that He will work all things together for his good."

"Therefore, I will seek to profit in this situation by asking of my brother in Christ to do me a favor. For to gain my adopted son by force and lose a fellow servant of the Lord, God forbid! If I do this right, who knows, I might gain his love the more, and he, in turn, will honor my request? If this is the will of the Father, this can only reinforce our relationship as well as save my beloved Onesimus, which is the true intent of this letter."

This Lesson covers: Phm 1:9

yet I prefer to appeal to you on the basis of love. It is as none other than Paul--an old man and now also a prisoner of Christ Jesus. (Phm 1:9)

DISCUSSION:

God is always after our hearts. He has written us love letters, and men have placed them in a book called the bible. The bible is for salvation first and then to mature us in every area of our lives. This will be a work in progress, but **never give up on the progress,** no matter how many times we fail to listen to that still soft voice of the Spirit.

Remember, the love of God is always operating, even when ours has fizzled out. He gives us His love so that we can love as His love works within us. As He works His love in us and through us, we learn of the gentleness and the strength His love provides.

Sure, God could come down from heaven. He could part the sky with thunder and lightning. He could raise another great prophet or re-establish another law, but what good is displaying power that He knows He already has and causes us to serve Him in fear rather than with a free-flowing genuine love? If you cannot freely love God, then it is lip/eye service that you offer Him. Where is your honest offering? It must be a free offering from the heart if you expect Him to receive it. And if He must give you something to get you to do something, then you do not truly understand how important it is to have God in your life. Nor do you have a genuine relationship with the Savior. And if you do not have it with His Son, you won't have it with the Father.

You may say, "Well, I have a covenant with Him, and He promises to bless me if I obey, and He promises to bless me because I believe in Jesus Christ." I agree with your statement, but I must tell you that if your heart is not right, you are falling short of loving God, and therefore, you are missing out on so much more that He is willing to give to you.

We both know that God will keep His promises. The question is, "can we keep our promises to Him?" Yes, we can by loving Him with all of our heart, soul, mind, and strength? Consider this one thing: He saved you from hell, which is enough of a blessing to last any man/woman for eternity. There will always be something running after our hearts. So, we must rely upon the Holy Spirit to prevent us from becoming a hostage of what chases us.

As the Apostle wrote his letter to Philemon, he used the fact that he was an old man to his advantage. He wants him to take into account that he is old. If he does so, then the Apostle is sure that Philemon will follow the customs of his people, and that is to give honor to all elders in the family.

My story version of verse: 1:9

"I am an old man, proclaims Paul, grant this old man possibly his last request. As you think of me, remember this old man is a prisoner for Christ. I have labored and suffered much for the gospel because I am His prisoner.

But I was willing to suffer that the gospel might be heard. May my labor continue to inspire servants like you, Philemon, who heard and received my message about Jesus Christ and how he died for our sins?

Out of all my years working for the goodness of my Savior, I have tried to reach every soul that I could. See, Philemon, I have come to appreciate the love of Jesus Christ and his purpose for dying on the cross. He did it so that no man would be lost unless he chose to reject Jesus. He died so that all men like Onesimus would know that they could approach Him for help. I know this to be true because I was once that lost man. I was unapproachable, but when Jesus spoke to me on the road of Damascus, my life changed.

"Being an old man, I needed a helper, and God sent Onesimus to me. See, I needed him just as much as he needed me. And in the end, Onesimus became my adopted son in the Lord, and I have become his earthly father, which he has never had."

Note:

Do you think this helped Philemon see why he kept Onesimus so long and why both men helped each other? The clearer the letter is, the likelihood Philemon will forgive and possibly release Onesimus.

ADDITION DISCUSSION: OLD MAN

The Apostle was asking Philemon to give in to him based on his service to the Lord and for the sacrifices that he made for the gospel. What an appealing argument. There is no denying that Paul has suffered for the gospel, and being an old man now, he is only asking a small favor for his loyalty to the church.

When you consider his efforts and what the Holy Spirit was able to do through the Apostle Paul, it makes it hard to say no to him. The Apostle continued his conversation, hoping that Philemon would reflect upon the fact that the Apostle was old and looking for maybe his last request.

This lesson covers the verse: Phm 1:10

> that I appeal to you for my son Onesimus,
> who became my son while I was in chains.
> (Phm 1:10)

DISCUSSION: SONSHIP

Surely this letter reveals the hearts of the Apostle and Onesimus. They beat as one. Paul wanted to do the right thing by sending Onesimus back, but it was clear how much he desired to free Onesimus and keep Philemon's friendship.

We should learn from this tug of war because it teaches us how we should try to bring about peace or the effort we should put forth to keep peace with our brothers. The Apostle has this great love for Onesimus, but he has to make sure that he gives Philemon the same amount of love and respect that will reflect the rights due to him.

Philemon has the right to have his property back. When we learn to love everyone and especially in the household of faith, we will see the Power of God in full operation on the earth. And His power will generate peace in a greater capacity, even in our personal lives.

This is what the Apostle was trying to convey in the letter. In fact, as the Apostle wrote, he expressed the idea that all three of them had hearts that beat for Christ. Therefore, if they have hearts for Christ, then they must have the same love for one another when it comes to all matters, including the ownership of Onesimus. As you strive towards becoming extraordinary, you must make sure that you keep the love of Christ in your heart for all men and in all situations that may arise.

The same role a father has for a son is the same role a mature Christian should have towards a babe in Christ. In the old world and probably in some foreign countries today, the oldest son is yet honored. He receives the most recognition. He is taught what is required to be the firstborn.

The oldest will eventually take care of all responsibilities towards the family. That includes all rules that were already set in place to secure and protect the family.

The land, the people, the finances, the animals are his responsibility. He carries the family forward when he reaches a certain age or after his father passes the family's authority to him. His whole life has been in preparation to take over the family. Everything he sees and touches would one day belong under his influence.

It was important to learn from the father what the family responsibility is. The leader must understand his role as the head of the family.

When Jesus was on the earth, he spoke to all his brothers and sisters about them being sons of God and that they had a responsibility toward the Kingdom. We receive the same message as we are taught by the Word of God what the Father expects from our lives. Those who surrender will be developed more and more into the likeness of Christ. That likeness develops you into that new man.

And every good father shall instruct their son or sons their responsibility as a man. Is that not what the Apostle was doing with Onesimus, teaching him about sonship, exposing him to The Word, and allowing the Holy Spirit to transform him. The Apostle knew one day Onesimus would help carry the message of the cross to the next generation. It is up to Philemon to be a part of building up Onesimus so that he knows what his responsibilities are towards the Kingdom of God.

Note:
 I speak of sons or sonship to describe how it worked in the Old Testament. This is not meant to exclude women but to highlight how Jewish families operated. Sonship can reference a woman just as the phrase "bride of Christ" represents a man.

The New Testament speaks of sonship in five scriptures, but the one I want you to understand is the one found in Ephesians 1:5. It tells that we were predestined for adoption to sonship through Jesus Christ. And Luke 20:36 supports the idea that we are sons of God because we have been born again. These two scriptures let us know that **we are all** sons of God. And we should not get hung up on the descriptions that appear to exclude a certain group.

Questions:

- Who is your spiritual father? Answer the question first and then read: Matt 23:8-10. Focus on the second part of verse eight.

- What does sonship look like to you?
  (Read: Rom 8:15,23; 9:4; Gal 4:5;
  Eph 1:5)

- Why are you called children of God?
  (Read: Rom 8:14; Gal 3:26)

PHILEMON'S HEART

As the Apostle Paul's letter takes root in Philemon's heart, he finds himself at a crossroads. Shall he embrace his newfound brother, or shall he punish his slave for running away?   I believe that this letter touched the hearts and lives of all three men. Let us try to discover what Philemon was thinking.

My story version of –The Heart

The battle of any decision starts in the heart of the person. Whatever the flesh dictates, actions follow, and whatever the spirit imposes, such actions also follow.

The question is, "what decision will be made when one comes to the crossroad of decision making?" One might say that their decision is based on which pathway appears to be the right one to take.

When Philemon turns to the left and views that path, it speaks to him like this: "I am the master and owner of Onesimus; therefore, whatever decision I make is the right." And when he turns to the other path, it says, "The better choice is this one because it is the path that requires forgiveness."

So, which is the better path, the selfish path where you stay in control of another soul, or shall you choose the path of love where you walk in forgiveness? We have all found ourselves at crossroads, but we have not always chosen the right road. The lesson that Philemon must come to terms with is that it is better to take the path that leads to love, forgiveness, and restoration.

Poor Philemon, by the time he receives this letter, Onesimus will be there. The pressure will be on, and he will have to make a quick decision as he stares Onesimus in the face.

As he reads the letter, the devil will remind him of Onesimus' crime and status in life. He will tell him that the punishment must equal the crime. And the Holy Spirit will speak to him as well, and say: "How important is it to make Onesimus an example before the other slaves?" Then Satan will counterattack and say: "If you do not punish Onesimus, you will appear weak in the eyes of your people." "But we know that the Holy Spirit will not remain quiet, and He will come against the evil that is being spoken into

106

the mind of Philemon. He would probably say, "To forgive is not a sign of weakness, Philemon, but of strength. True love requires strength because you have decided to love in spite of it.   Resist the enemy and the appearance of weakness."

"It does not matter what the ungodly man would say or think, but what matters is that you show the love of Christ in all situations." Kindness will shame those who originally felt you should punish rather than forgive. They will eventually say, "If he can forgive a slave who has done him wrong, surely, he will forgive me of those things that I have done wrong against him."

"Can you handle the pressure of how you may be judged by your righteous decision? If you can, then you are on the road to becoming exceptional.

"This is what Christ has done for all men. He died so that men who believed in him could love their neighbor completely. They would love even those who did not deserve love. Christ died for all and in spite of our sinful nature.   "Oh, Philemon, Satan is after your heart. Oh, Philemon, you are being tested once again to see what your heart will reveal? Will the real Philemon please stand up?"

DISCUSSION: OBEDIENCE

The Apostle is aware, as Philemon is aware, that forgiveness is an act of obedience, and it demonstrates that you are truly a son of God. (71) The right spirit will not demand satisfaction, nor will one lose control and beat their slave for voluntarily returning.

King David once said, "search my heart O' God and place in me a clean heart…spirit; if there is any anxiousness there, remove it and put in me a clean heart." (72) In most cases, a mature Christian knows how to control anxiety.

Yes, it may rise up, but it can be pulled down. We must cast down every imagination that tries to exhaust itself above the Word of God. (73) And as we master control of our spirit through the knowledge of God, we are elevating ourselves to a higher level of living.

The word "knowledge" [Strong's G1108] entails things that are lawful and unlawful for Christians. It is about moral wisdom/right living. It is the knowledge of our religion. (74) This knowledge that we are given comes through the Word of God.

That Word is perfect, and it provides us with wisdom from on high. That wisdom is why some people are called to do great things for God.

Thus, blessings follow those who will live an extraordinary life. The flesh will always fight to be on top, and we shall always be fighting to suppress it. For we are dead in Christ, meaning our flesh is under the authority of our spirit man. We give the flesh no authority; therefore, it acts as if it is dead. When the flesh is dead, there can be no retaliation.

Our flesh will never stop bucking and demanding its way. Philemon's flesh wants him to be angry with Onesimus, and Philemon's flesh will give him reasons why he has that right. But we must be able to decide if it is sound reasoning to become angry. Whether you know or not, The Word says: "to be slow to anger." It says we do not allow your anger to continue past sundown. (75)

Philemon must decide if Paul has a right to ask such a great favor from him. He must decide how he will control his other slaves if he should grant compassion to Onesimus. He must consider whether he wants the blessing of God or the cursing that will come from not forgiving. But doesn't all decisions end with a choice, and does not all choices lead to cursing or a blessing?

Philemon will have a lot to figure out what he must do. May he have an ear to hear what the Holy Spirit will say to him when he is confronted?

My story version of: New Man

The new man has a voice too, and he would instruct Philemon wisely. His mind would have a conversation with his new spirit:

You know Paul is right. This is the time to display love, just as God showed love towards me when I was in sin. I remember when Paul taught me that God will not hear my prayers of forgiveness if I did not forgive, and especially to those who ask of me." (76)

The new man's voice would say, "Philemon, Oh, Philemon, forgiveness is right here; you need to reach out and grab it if you want to please, the Father. A wise man does not weigh his decision to forgive based on what someone has done to them, but he bases it upon the same love that he received from Christ when he walked in the error of his ways."

"Let his commandments outweigh your anger. When you focus on forgiveness based on the forgiveness you received from God, it makes forgiving so much easier. Here is your formula: Compare Onesimus, one sin against your sins,

Philemon. You will see that there is no comparison, for your sins are greater when you look at your past, present, and future mistakes."

Questions:

- How often do you find yourself getting mad or getting offended? (Read: Jas 1: 19-20; Prov 10:19,13:3 18:13, 21:12; Eph 4:31)

- If others exam your character, what would be revealed about you – something new or something you already know? (Read: Psa 101:2; Isa 43:18, 93; 2 Cor 5:17; Luk 11:41,8:15)

A bright future with Christ is a person who has mastered long-suffering, patience, and kindness. (77) And if you have not mastered them, do not give up. There is power in The Word of God to make you an over-comer.

DISCUSSION: THE ORDER

It is clear to the Apostle that he is counting on the love and respect that Philemon has for him. This letter should make him think long and hard. It will cause him to reflect on how God operates, and it is clear as a bell that God was working in Onesimus from Colossae to Rome and from Rome to the Apostle's home. Philemon must be careful that he does not find himself fighting against the will of God.

Paul is surely suggesting that Philemon take a moment to see God's hand directing Onesimus' life. Who can tell what God is doing unless He reveals His action to them? Rarely do we see Him in action, but we **see the results of His presence**. And if God chooses to work, by allowing Onesimus to run from Philemon into the arms of the Apostle Paul, so be it!

Maybe there was a spec in Philemon's eye that needed to be removed so that other slaves could be saved. Could Philemon have held a tight range as a slave-master, or did he overlook them and did not count them in as potential converts.

One cannot claim to love God and show favoritism between his friends and neighbors, believers and non-believers, slaves, and bondservants. If we knew the blessings behind love, everyone would jump at the opportunity to love their neighbor.

Does the heart of Philemon have the ability to expand itself? Will he be able to read between the lines of the Apostle's words, which explain that these things did not happen by osmosis? This was an act of God reaching out to Onesimus, Philemon, and the Apostle Paul as well?

Can a master and follower of God believe a change can come on a useless slave? It is one thing to proclaim yourself changed, but it weighs more when someone else declares it for you. And with ink and paper, the great Apostle Paul confirms there has been a change in Onesimus.

Questions:

- Has God knitted your heart to a younger disciple? (Read: Matt 5:16, 28:19 NLT; Prov 9:9; 1 Cor 4:17)

- Do you see them as your adopted son or daughter? (Read: Mk 16:15)

- How would you extend yourself to protect your adopted child? (Read: Jhn 15:13)

STAGE FOUR

This lesson covers: Phm 1:11-12

Formerly he was useless to you, but now he has become useful both to you and to me. (Phm 1:11)

I am sending him--who is my very heart— back to you. (Phm 1:12)

DISCUSSION :

Now let us examine verses 11-12. The Apostle Paul unveils a negative image that Philemon has about Onesimus. He asks Philemon to take another look at his slave and <u>see him as his brother</u> in the Lord.

He tells him that a natural man cannot discern the potential of another man unless God reveals it. There are men who have a hidden value that is yet to be revealed.

The former things of a new believer have nothing to do with the future of that person once God has taken control. Because when a man receives salvation,

114

the old things are gone, and he becomes a new creature in Christ. Onesimus is now a new creature in Christ, and Philemon must be made aware of this change and accept it.

Sometimes this is what we all have to do, take another look even if the first experience was disastrous. You never know when a man will find Christ, but if you continue to close your mind to him, you will never see that new man come forth. Does this help you to see how important it is to forgive?

You may also miss the opportunity to serve with that new believer. Barnabus understood that, and he was the first to befriend Paul. Barnabus worked with Paul, and they accomplished great things for the Lord. He helped the other disciples to accept Paul and what a blessing Paul became for the church of Christ. The main thing you must remember, there is no room for hatred and love. When we harbor both; we leave room for failure to come in and destroy the greatness that is trying to operate through you.

My story version of verse: Treasure

Paul would say, "The real treasure hidden inside Onesimus has been uncovered. His true potential has benefitted me the entire time he has been in Rome. My bonds have been more tolerable since we found one another. Therefore, I ask you, my co-worker in the Lord, can one

115

find value in a useless slave? I can say for sure, yes. Through God, all things are possible.

Through the Spirit of Christ, death is swallowed up and replaced with new life. Poverty turns to prosperity, and uselessness is exchanged for usefulness. The transformation that takes place in Christ makes the former things pass away, and it brings forth the new." (78)

"Out of all the men that day in my home, it was the Spirit that led me to him. A useless runaway slave, and it was that same Spirit that divulged to me that his soul was chosen by God. Imagine the hundreds of thousands of wandering souls in Rome, but God wanted Onesimus.

I quickly approached him and then laid hands upon him and spoke over his life. And he responded with sweet submissiveness and a confession that Jesus is Lord." "Now, the man that you once called and known as useless is no longer that man, but he is useful. He has taken up his cross, and he is following Christ. He has placed his affection upon me and has been a godsend from that day forth. Oh, how my heart rejoiced in the Lord, for
God had sent me a helper in my bondage."

"I can accomplish just as much being bound in my home as I did as a free man. Onesimus is my feet where I cannot go physically, and he is my eyes and mouth where I send him. He has encouraged me as I have encouraged him Oh Philemon, you have won yourself a prize servant…a gift from God."

"Shall we not praise God for turning his life around? Let us lift our voice unto the Lord, who can make the impossible possible. He recreates a new mind and a new heart and puts a right spirit in a man."

"What I have seen and what I have heard, and what I know today about Onesimus is that when he hears his name, his efforts match with the meaning of his name, "useful." (79)

Questions

- Do you feel that the Apostle is challenging Philemon to exam his heart to make more room for love? Am I challenging your heart today?

- To ask for forgiveness for a worthless slave who has run away is a lot. Do you agree or not? Would you please discuss your reasoning with the group?

- What should Philemon do with his troublemaking property, which is returning home?

- What about the item he stole when
  he ran away. Would you make him
  pay it back, and how would you
  accomplish that task?

This lesson covers: Phm 1:12

  I am sending him--who is my very
  heart—back to you. (Phm 1:12)

DISCUSSION: TRUTH REVEALED

Now the time has come for the Apostle to disclose the true meaning of his letter. He tells Philemon that he has his property and that Onesimus has been with him for a while. How do you think Philemon will respond to this information? Will he be relieved to know that Onesimus was found?

Or will he be offended that the Apostle has kept this secret from him? The bible does not tell us how long Onesimus stayed with the Apostle before he decided to go back home. But I would guess that Philemon would have appreciated it if the Apostle had told him where Onesimus was when they connected in Rome. You also have to wonder why the Apostle Paul chose not to tell Philemon until now. Onesimus left with the reputation of a useless slave, but now

Philemon's property value, which is Onesimus, has doubled. His value has increased because God is now in his life.

A change has taken over, and the useless/ unregenerate man has been regenerated. He now sees life differently, and the servant slave who resisted and argued and stirred up trouble is coming back to serve Philemon with the approval of the Apostle Paul. Onesimus knows that he must serve Philemon with singleness of heart, and he is willing.

Strong's word: "singleness" G573 in the Blue Letter Bible implies "with sincerity, without dissimulation or self-seeking." Therefore, the Apostle Paul is saying serve your master as if you are serving God. Always keep your mind on God and how you can please Him. We are representatives of Christ, and thus we have to walk out that life where everyone can see.

If we work hard, obey, God will be please because we are showing the world that God lives within us, and it is He…God, that completes our joy. This type of lifestyle would be contagious. It would draw the attention of others, and therefore, they would see the Christ in you without saying one word.

It may shame those who watch the unveiling of the new man. They watch to see if he will continue to be sincere. If one can be a great

119

representative of Christ, the watchers may come to accept Christ also. Remember, every time the Word tells us how to live, and we apply it to our lives, we are happier for it. We give glory to God, and we draw others to Christ. Power is not always revealed by destroying something. Sometimes power can be quiet as a man living his life in peace before the Lord.

My story version of verse: 1:12

"I cannot wait to hear from you, for I know you will be sending me a good report of what you now see in my adopted son, Onesimus. I am sending back to you your slave, who is also my heart. Take care of my heart Philemon as I know that he will take care of you."

"I know that Onesimus will serve your correctly because he has a new spirit, and he has shown himself faithful in serving me. He will do the same for you once he has returned home." "For Onesimus will be profitable because he no longer sees himself as a slave, as someone's property, although he is still your property Philemon."

"The mind of Christ dwells in every believer, Philemon. And every godly mindset that produces fruit is produced by the power of God. When your spirit and soul are free from the bondage of this world, you can be in a lion's den like Daniel, and you will not fear. God will bring you out and bring you forth. Onesimus' mind is set on God, and he seeks to know more."

"Our faith tells us that from our own experiences that God is operating in what we believe to be a dreadful situation. No one would want to go back into slavery after tasting the goodness of God and the freedom that comes from His love. "But when the enemy cries out, "Slave," our faith will remind us... that we are not bound by the titles given to us nor the situation we face. This is what I have been teaching Onesimus so that he is prepared to return home."

"Do you know that this is how great men of God accomplish their calling? They did not see themselves as slaves; thus, they were <u>not limited</u> to what they could do. If we see ourselves as slaves, then we connect ourselves to a title that God has not given us."

Remember the story of David and Goliath? Do you think David would have had the right spirit to fight Goliath if he reminded himself that he was the youngest man in the camp? He did not change his thoughts even when he discovered he could not wear the king's armor. The only thing that mattered was the fact that God was with him."

DISCUSSION: GOD

Paul knows God, and therefore, he trusts that God is sending a breakthrough that will move Philemon's heart. The Apostle envisioned Onesimus' life filled with doing work for the Lord. He probably imagined Onesimus working in the church that meets at Philemon's house. As a servant, he could inspire other slaves to be honest and trustworthy. When you become a new creature in Christ, the possibilities are endless.

When we examine our past, we see that we were not useful, nor were we beneficial to the Kingdom of God. We were not useful to anyone because we worked for things that would benefit us. But that is not how God saw us then nor now. He sees those things that be not as though they were. (80) He sees your hidden potential. He anoints your gifts and talents because they are beneficial to His plan.

Every believer is a miracle, for God took uselessness and turned us into useful servants of God. You may feel that you are as invisible as Eve, who at one point had no physical body, yet God called Adam "he them." (81) When He spoke to Adam, He was also talking to her.

Her physical body had not yet been created, but she yet existed in the mind of God. And when it

122

comes to us, He sees you, even before you were formed in your mother's womb. (82) He called us forth to be children of God. He called us because He foreknew that one day we would become "useful."

Be intentional about your life and what you are going to do for the Kingdom of God. And do not let anyone tell you to put out the flame that He placed in you. No, you may not become a TV evangelist. You may not grow into the greatest author or speaker. Yet, surrendering under the power of God and being intentional each day to serve Him in some capacity will open up new opportunities that you never thought would manifest. It causes the abundant life given by Christ to illuminate your mind, your gifts, your ability to love, and your territory.

Eventually, Philemon will come to realize that Onesimus has added usefulness to his character. One day he will see the greatness in Onesimus unfold. As Philemon reads his letter, he will be wondering what the Apostle did to have such an impact upon Onesimus' life. But the Apostle only had a small part in Onesimus going from ordinary to extraordinary. It was God indwelling in Onesimus that made the true change in Onesimus' character and lifestyle.

Here is how I perceive the thoughts that went through Philemon's mind as he continued to read his letter. "What could have happened in Rome that makes the Apostle Paul so sure about this ungrateful slave of mine? The Apostle refers to Onesimus as his heart! He says that Onesimus is obedient! This doesn't sound like my slave, Onesimus to me, thought Philemon."

"Then the Holy Spirit began to show him his own life, which helped turn Philemon's mind to what God can do. "Maybe he has truly changed. I know I did when I was born again. Oh, the mystery that lies in the power of God."

"There must have been a change because I know the Apostle as well as he knows me, and I know he has a low tolerance for fearful/useless people who lay their cross down for the sake of the flesh. I recall the breakup of Paul and Barnabus due to the immature John Mark." (83)

"I heard that the Holy Spirit called Paul and Barnabus out to work as a team. John Mark was invited to go with them on their first missionary trip. (84) They said while the men were in Perga of Pamphylia, John Mark packed it all up and returned to Jerusalem. (85)

By the time, the two men were ready to go on their second missionary trip, Barnabus told Paul that he wanted to try John Mark again. He felt

John Mark deserved a second chance, but Paul would not hear of it. The disagreement was so strong that this "great team" split up. (86) They say that Barnabas took John Mark and headed to Cyprus. and Paul took Silas and went to Cilicia." (87) "Whatever caused John Mark to turn and head for home was enough for Paul to believe he was not ready to serve. So, I have to believe that the Apostle would not lie about Onesimus."

MORE DISCUSSION:

We see that Paul and Barnabus were good friends until Paul judged John Mark by his actions. It is later on that we learn when Paul needed support, he asked for John Mark. John Mark had a gift that needed nurturing, and obviously, he got it from Barnabus. At the right time, he blossomed into a great man of faith that the Apostle Paul had to recognize.

This is what the Apostle wants for Onesimus and Philemon. He wants Philemon to give him a chance, which is something that Paul did not do for John Mark until much later. How many times have we seen great partnerships in the Kingdom, running at full capacity to find that Satan has come in and broken up a beautiful partnership? Yes, everyone is yet saved, but the power that was working in harmony has diminished. It has diminished because Barnabus is headed in one direction, and Paul is going in another. When they were together, their power was able to send ten thousand to flight. (88) Do you see the diminished value because the partnership is broken?

Therefore, the Apostle Paul understood the importance of a second chance. Now he is trying to prevent Philemon from missing the extra power he could have if he would accept Onesimus. Both Paul and Barnabus learned a valuable lesson. It is good to be bold, but there are times compassion for another is just what the fearful need to become fearless. And too much empathy can cripple a man from maturing. The two men balance the other one out. It takes boldness and compassion to work in and for the Kingdom of God.

Trying to place blame on Philemon for the reason Onesimus ran is like trying to decide if the boldness of Paul or the compassion of Barnabus should come first. Maturity is developed with time; if we have the patience to watch it grow. And when maturity has evolved and the fruit of the Spirit is produced, one will find plenty of boldness and compassion on the tree to pluck.

In time, John Mark reached his maturity level, and it was the Apostle Paul who requested him by name. I love what the Apostle said, "send him to me because he is helpful to my ministry. (89) The Apostle understood that sometimes we have

126

to take a second look at those who appear useless. I believe that Onesimus became as useful to Philemon as John Mark became useful to Paul.

So let us take another look at verse eleven. What is a useful believer? A useful believer is one whom the Holy Spirit has control over. The believer has become aware of their gift/talent and understands how important it is to turn their lives and their gifts over to the Spirit to use as he sees fit.

Thus, the anointing will flow between the Spirit and the believer's spirit, and the power of God will flow outwardly from that believer. Others will be blessed because of their faith in Jesus Christ.

The Body of Christ:

When we become believers in Christ, we are assigned to a part of the Body. Therefore, if they become a leg, they can support the Body of Christ the way they never did before. It appears that Onesimus was the legs because he carried the message of Christ for the Apostle Paul, and later in another chapter, he brought a letter to the Colossae.

Then what makes a person exceptional? You become exceptional when you are n Christ, and you are working under the **anointing** while in your **proper place** in the Body of Christ. There is no other combination that works the way God has ordained it.

In the Kingdom, every piece is special. There are delicate pieces, and other parts are durable, but when they help form The Body of Christ, The Body becomes a powerful weapon against Satan and his demons. The Body runs on love, and it is the love we have for one another that causes us to work in harmony. Therefore, the Apostle can say that Onesimus is useful; he is useful for the Kingdom for he is now a part of that Kingdom.

It took the journey from Colossae to Rome for Onesimus to find what he longed for; he needed to discover the true man. Therefore, God led him to Rome. Who else kept him safe while running and living as a free man? Who was it that protected him on the dangerous highway from Colossae to Rome, but God

It was God who led Onesimus to Paul by keeping Paul under house arrest so the two men would connect? God's timing is impeccable.

Questions:

- How are you helping The Body of Christ? (Read: Rom 7:3; Eph 4:11-13)

128

- Do you operate in love, which is the Glue that holds us all together. Examine your heart to make sure you do not hold anything against anyone. (Read: 2 Cor 3:5-7,11; Eph 5;2)

Name some things you feel the men had to earn. Here is what I have learned about this story:

Paul:
o He has learned to give a man a second look.

o He turned a death ear to the temptation of using his authority against Philemon.

o He had to learn that no matter how much you want to defend and protect someone, it has to be done in love and faith in God's ability to fix the issue.

Philemon:

o He had to learn to love unconditionally.

o He learned not to judge people based on their appearance or significance in life.

o He learned that God chooses the candidate.

o He learned that he must always show compassion, forgiveness and not worry about what others think.

Onesimus:

o He has learned that a man can change his stars if he put his trust in God.

o He has learned that God will put people in your path to help you fix the brokenness inside.

o He has learned that God has no favorites, that all are equal in the Kingdom of God.

o He has learned that focusing on Christ will elevate your mind and remove worries.

STAGE FIVE

The Lesson verses: Phm 1:13-14

I would have liked to keep him with me so That he could take your place in helping me while I am in chains for the gospel. (Phm 1:13)

But I did not want to do anything without your consent so that any favor you do would not seem forced but would be voluntary. (Ph 1:14)

The Lesson verse: Phm 1:13

I would have liked to keep him with me so that he could take your place in helping me while I am in chains for the gospel. (Phm 1:13)

DISCUSSION:

The Apostle puts Philemon's mind at ease when he acknowledges that Onesimus is Philemon's slave and not Paul's to do as he pleases. We have people today who borrow lawn equipment from their neighbors. They keep the item so long that the borrower believes that the thing now belongs to them.

131

When the borrower recognizes that the property belongs to the lender, the lender is now at ease because he does not have to prove that the item belongs to him. It was clear to see that in this case, the Apostle is not the lender.

Sure, Onesimus was happy and contented where he was; the Apostle Paul was grateful for the excellent student that Onesimus had become and for the son that the Apostle needed. Still, there came a time Paul had to recall that he had his neighbor's property, and thus, it was time to return him, regardless of how great the need to keep him. Onesimus did not want to break fellowship with the Apostle, and the Apostle did not wish to break the connection with Philemon, but for peace to remain, an account to Philemon was necessary.

When we operate in love, when we start off humble, and when we have an open heart to put our brother first, things always work out. It works out because we are allowing the Holy Spirit to lead. The Apostle, led by the Holy Spirit, openly admits, "This is your property, Philemon." He is acknowledging that Philemon is the rightful owner of the slave called Onesimus.

My story version of verse: 1:13

"I have kept your slave because he has been a blessing to me while I have been under house arrest. Forgive me, Philemon, for I meant no harm: I had no intentions of keeping him as long

132

as I did. He has been such a great help to me that I forgot who he belongs to.

Now that I have been reminded by the Holy Spirit that Onesimus belongs to; I can no longer keep him. But the work that Onesimus has been doing here in Rome, I can say, that he belongs to God, Philemon, and then to you. I write asking for forgiveness for two reasons. First for me, using your property as if it were mine and then for him running away.

"To tell you the truth, I would love to keep him while I remain in chains. He supports me the way you used to when we were together. You understand my ministry, and you know the necessary things, and now Onesimus has taken on those duties. God bless him!"

Now that he is returning home, I need to know that this man is going to be okay coming back home. I want to speak from my heart so that you can begin to understand the relationship and the love I have found knowing Onesimus." He has a hunger to know the Lord. This hunger is so authentic that I began to have private sessions with him. It is exciting to be around new converts. Their energy and thirst for the Word cause excitement to stir up in me."

The Lesson verse: Phm 1:14

But I did not want to do anything without your consent so that any favor you do would not seem forced but would be voluntary. (Phm 1:14)

DISCUSSION :

First, we must review the Apostle's first statement in verse fourteen. He said that he did not want to do anything without Philemon's consent. Here are my three questions for you to consider?

1. How long do you think Onesimus has been with Paul? Does the length of time matter?

2. Do you think that the Apostle should have sought consent the moment he found out that Onesimus belonged to Philemon?

3. Is it fitting for the Apostle to ask or make a remark that he wanted Onesimus to stay with him? Especially since he knew that Onesimus was a runaway.

It is nice that the Apostle is seeking Philemon's permission, but if he knew from the beginning that Onesimus was Philemon's runaway, then he has crossed the line. Maybe he saw Onesimus as a godsend where he could be used to help him in his ministry because he is now a part of The Body.

134

To have a healthy relationship, one should never demand a favor but give the friend the opportunity, without pressure, to say yes or no to that favor. God does the same thing with us. He offers His love, and He asks for our love on a volunteer basis. A healthy friendship allows each party to speak what is in their hearts without rejection. This healthy fear of friendship is based on truth and mutual respect for one another's opinions. It is a terrible thing catering to a friend, who can only see what matters most to them.

Friendship is not having someone agree with you on everything. Besides, how can iron sharpen iron if one party is prevented from sharpening the other?

The Apostle's request is sincere and needful, yet the request is not considering that Onesimus ran away. He has stolen from his master without reconciling with him. Would it be inappropriate to allow him to stay in Rome when he has been disobedient? It is not recommended that one should reward bad behavior.

It is better that Onesimus return home and set things right. On the other side of this issue, we must respect Philemon. He just found out where his slave has been all this time. He also thinks that his personal friend has kept this secret from him.

This may be the reason the Apostle made his request the way he did. He knew what Philemon would be thinking. Yet, he asked this big favor.

I must commend the Apostle for leaving the decision to Philemon what is the best thing to do.

The Apostle was right in his actions because he had taken liberty earlier by keeping Onesimus in Rome with him. Could he have also been gracious because he would be asking Philemon for a few more considerations? In spite of what he should have done from the beginning, the Apostle is trying to make amends by allowing Philemon the right to say no and to assure him that there will be no repercussions from Paul. Therefore, a friend may ask a favor, but only the mature ones will ask, placing no pressure on the friendship.

My story version of verse: 1:14

"Although I speak of my needs, and I speak of his usefulness, towards them, I do not want to override your authority. Therefore, I ask a favor, so you may have a free and clear mind to choose what you think is best to oversee Onesimus' future.

If it is better that he stays with you than me, then I agree with it." If you are wondering, do I have a right to get involved in your decision, I will answer, "yes, I do." My heart is tied up in this situation,

Philemon, because I love Onesimus like any father would love his son. I am interested in his

136

life because he is now a believer, and I am an overseer of the churches."

"I have written to the church about the conduct of a slave. I said that every slave is bound serve their master. However, serving requires having the heart to help versus serving with "eye service" only. (90) No man wants a servant who can only do the right thing when supervised."

Paul understood what God required. his is why he said to Philemon, "if you think it is best...I am in agreeance with whatever your decision is." The Apostle was honoring Philemon's rights as the owner and the final decision-maker. Let him continue with his plea:

"But Philemon, I have also taught that a <u>master must be merciful to his slaves</u>. God is not pleased when we are cruel to one another. Our God set His commands so that peace rules, but both parties must be willing to obey.

"Every creature of God is under His control. We must open our eyes and see the possibility in all of God's creatures, even if they are slaves. God, your Master, is not a respecter of person, Philemon. Thus, we are not to exhaust one person over another. We must open our eyes and <u>see the possibility in all of God's creatures,</u> even if they are slaves."

"It is true that a slave has no right to run away nor to steal from their master, and if he has done this sin, and he has, but that sin has led him to Christ, then thank God for all things work together for the good of those who love Him." (101)

"Remember what it was like to be new in Christ? You have come a long way yourself, Philemon. Do you remember what you were like before accepting Jesus as Lord? **I do**, and yet I walked you through your confession of faith. I have already said that you and I are co-workers in Christ. I see the words and commitment to the Kingdom in your in your actions. I know just one look upon Onesimus' face will cause you to change your heart and set you both free. This is what I am working to accomplish by letter."

"Know that my request consists of you being willing to see things my way, thus adding no pressure on you because of the mantle I carry. Please see this as one brother making a request to another. I am mature enough to be content no matter what the outcome is. (102) Rest assured, my friend, and let your decision be a free one."

Questions

- How successful are you in trusting God with the right outcome? (Read Prov 3:5-6)

138

- When you have asked a friend for a favor, how did you manage it when they said no? Or did they say yes because they felt pressured. (Read: Eph 4:1-2; Luk 11; 5-9)

- If you were Onesimus, would you return home with no guarantees? (Read: Job 12:10)And why was it time for Onesimus to go home? (Read: Eccl 3:1)

- How would you treat your slave and brother? (Read: 1 Corinthians 13:1-13) Do you show true love towards them? (Read: Matt 22:37; Eph 4:32)

  - How should a master reconcile with his slave? (Read: Gal 6:10)

STAGE SIX

This lesson covers: Phm 1:15-17

Perhaps the reason he was separated from you for a little while was that you might have him back forever – (Phm 1:15)

no longer as a slave, but better than a slave, as a dear brother. He is very dear to me but even dearer to you, both as a fellow man and as a brother in the Lord. (Phm 1:16)

So, if you consider me a partner, welcome him as you would welcome me. (Phm 1:15- 17)

This lesson verse: Phm 1:15

Perhaps the reason he was separated from you for a little while was that you might have him back forever— (Phm 1:15)

DISCUSSION :

The Apostle is suggesting that Philemon should think about why God allowed Onesimus to run away. Could it be that God had a purpose for the separation? I would say he certainly did. He

140

needed to get Onesimus to a man who would present Christ to him. He needed a man that would be patient and understanding and be like a father to him. And we know that man to be Apostle Paul.

When the right time comes, God will honor Philemon's right to have Onesimus back. God will be involved in this situation until it works freely for both men. He will either send Onesimus back, allowing Philemon to change his heart and release him to the Apostle. Or He will bless Onesimus right there in Philemon's backyard.

But right now, God needed Onesimus' attention. Thus, He placed him in a strange and unfriendly town. He knew that if his back were against the wall, he would cry out to Him. It is sad but true; most believers would not have turned to God if all continued to go well. There is something about suffering…suffering alone that causes one to look up or reach out to others.

What was important to Onesimus was the fact he was a free man, and he was living on his own terms. Once the Apostle Paul converted him, Onesimus would need someone to expound on the Word in order for him to grow. And as he understood his relationship with God, it would settle his rebellious spirit because he would know that he does not have to fight to survive.

He would learn that he could rely upon God to meet all his needs.

While Onesimus was learning, Philemon was growing as well. The Holy Spirit was working on Philemon about the way Onesimus was treated. He was also working on Philemon about the treatment of all his slaves. During the time of separation, it gave Philemon a chance to reflect on how he should care for his slaves. And I am sure the spirit revealed to him that even his slaves were potential servants of God.

Once both men were ready to appreciate the other, God would send Onesimus back home, and that would bring peace. For Onesimus, there would be peace because his master would respect him as a believer.

Philemon would have regained his property and received him back better than before. He would also have peace once he could see that Onesimus was now a changed man with a desire to serve God at home or in Rome.

It is a blessing from God to receive something back that is in better working order than when you loan it out. That is how you know that God is involved; He can fix anything if we give, Him time to work things out the way He sees it. I am sure there are slave owners who think beating the slave will make him act or perform better. But what will eventually happen is that they will either kill the slave or kill their spirit by beating them. And if they are dead or beaten down, you will have lost hundreds of dollars from their death and the loss of productivity.

Man's way of thinking will always make the matter worst. God's way solves the problem for both sides. His commandments show love and respect for the slave and the master. If Philemon does not believe in the possibility of a changed man/slave, it will not matter what Onesimus does when he returns. Philemon will continue to see him as he was. It takes faith in God and love in one's heart to see **a man** and see **his worth**.

Have you ever been in a conversation where a particular name comes up? No matter how positive the discussion was about that person, someone will bring up their past? The negative person refuses to see the good in the changed person. This unforgiving person still lives in the past and has bound himself to it. He can only see the old character of the man even though the conversation is about the new man.

Unforgiveness binds a man to the past, and forgiveness releases him. We pray that Philemon will not become the negative, unforgiving man. It would be a shame to see Onesimus being set free while Philemon is yet in bondage from the past. What could Philemon think as he reads that his slave, who ran away, is now a believer in Christ? Will this surprise him with excitement,

143

or will this additional good news go over his head?

There are times; our minds are so consumed with a particular part of a problem that when other details are given, we cannot hear nor understand what has been said. They cannot hear it or comprehend it because they are stuck on a piece of the story. Philemon might be so stuck on the fact that Onesimus stole and ran away that he does not hear that he is now a servant of the Lord.

Letting go of unforgiveness and unlocking yourself from the past opens additional possibilities of a brighter future. Always be ready to accept new revelation from God.

Questions:

• Are you a slave to something hindering your elevation?

• Have you ever had to separate yourself from someone for a season?

• Have you reconciled with that person?

This lesson verse: Phm 1:16

no longer as a slave, but better than a slave, as a dear brother. He is very dear to me but even dearer to you, both as a fellow man and as a brother in the Lord. (Phm 1:16)

DISCUSSION:

Paul says that Onesimus is no longer a slave, but he is a brother…a dear brother in the Lord. If he is a brother, and he is, then how should Philemon see this convert? Can Philemon look upon Onesimus the slave and see Onesimus, my brother? **How does a master reconcile with his slave?** He does this by acknowledging him as a brother.

How does he acknowledge him and balance the difference? If Philemon sees him as a slave, he has a right to put him to work in his field or barn or wherever he needs him. And if he can see Onesimus as a brother, how shall he conduct himself when he needs him to work? Can you see him as your property and yet treat him as an equal? It appears impossible to do both.

Maybe he has to start slow. Meaning he should make sure that he is kind to his slave as he makes demands on things that he needs Onesimus to do. When Sunday comes, all slaves should attend service if they wish. And when they arrive, they should welcome them into the house of the Lord. If Onesimus begin to operate in the Spirit, can Philemon respect him?

I understood that Onesimus no longer sees himself as a slave, and he acts like a man, full of the Holy Spirit. And because of his conversion, when Onesimus' gift is in use, Philemon must resist his flesh. For it will surely try to take charge as the master and pastor of the church. He must respect his gift because it is of the Lord.

I like the phrase where he references Onesimus as a dear brother, but what is more eye-catching is that the Apostle says that he is dear to Philemon in two ways?

He is dear as a fellow man and then as a brother in the Lord. I notice that the Apostle did not call Onesimus a slave but a fellow man and a brother. Could this be the Apostles' way of saying to Philemon that he must see Onesimus as a man and a brother in Christ and no longer a slave? These two words [fellow man/brother] give new meaning to Onesimus status. It makes him human and places him into the world with the rest of the church people.

Paul hopes that Philemon becomes partners with him in a new arena. He is already a partner with the Apostle in the church, but now Paul is expecting Philemon to become a partner with him in the development of Onesimus. There is a need for every believer to invest in their brothers and sisters in Christ. The Lord commands us to help one another to grow and to become the best there is. He informs Philemon that he has already welcomed Onesimus and has accepted him as a brother, now he lays the decision at Philemon's feet to do the same.

My story version of verse: 1:16

Onesimus is thinking to himself, and this is what I imagine taking place in his mind: "None of us are slaves, but brothers and sisters in Christ. Only slaves are bound because they serve at the lowest level, and they answer to the master's call. A slave's life is in the hands of one man or one family, and if anyone of them chooses to be cruel, the slave has no choice but to suffer."

"And if the master is a slave to something or has an addiction, then the master is in bondage like the slave. But this is not my issue, for my master is a God-fearing man, says Onesimus. If Philemon has any bondage, he is a bondservant to the Lord Jesus Christ.

"And when I return home, there will be opportunities to show Philemon that I am a changed man. I realize that I cannot force him to see me, but I will allow my hard work and my gifts to make room for me. As the Apostle said, my dedication to my master will please the Lord, and my gift will benefit the church. I am indeed

147

a blessed man. I will be even more blessed when all things that are working together for my good come to completion for me and my master, Philemon."

"I am my master's brother, and I have rights and privileges that he must honor as well as I must honor his right as my master. May God help me keep my eyes on Him and allow Him to be the God of my life?

When His will comes to past, then Philemon will be my brother in the Lord more than my earthly master. For I am as my adopted father says, I too am a prisoner of Christ".

Questions

- How do you think Onesimus became dear to the Apostle Paul? What kind of helper could he have been to him?

- Have you ever been under the control of a strong-will person, explain?

This lesson verse: Phm 1:17

So, if you consider me a partner, welcome him as you would welcome me. (Phm 1:15-17)

DISCUSSION:

The Apostle sums up his thoughts, and he writes. This time he challenged Philemon to welcome Onesimus as he would welcome him.

This could be the hardest thing that is asked of Philemon in the letter. Surely Paul is kidding, whoever heard of a slave owner welcoming a slave as if he carried the same importance as the Apostle Paul? He chuckled, I sure, as he read the statement again. The Apostle was sincere and serious that all brethren are equal in Christ: there is no Jew, Greek, Gentile, male, female, bondservant, nor maiden, but we are all one in Christ. (103) And I am also confident that he stood on the idea that God is not a respecter of persons. (104)

Either way, he gave Philemon a great deal to absorb. Any man that claims he is a believer of Christ must put away his childish practices. We do not have the authority to choose who can be in the Body of Christ, but we can fix our attitudes so that we see all people as God does. We must also learn to forgive and present the gospel wherever there is an opportunity. Prejudice is a hindrance to the Kingdom of God.

149

How should a master <u>welcome a runaway slave</u>? The Apostle was instructing as he made this request. He was saying, search your heart and see what you find. Can you, Philemon, accept Onesimus as a brother, although he is your slave? If Philemon never considered his servants as a candidate for Christianity, then we can be sure Philemon was failing as a leader.

The Apostle touched where most men place their value, money, and friendship. He tells Philemon, if you value our partnership in the Lord, welcome him back like a brother in Christ, and begin to see him as a brother and no longer property you owned to trade or sell.

The Apostle was not trying to take away his rights to own slaves, for Onesimus is indeed his property. Philemon is being challenged to love harder and deeper than he ever has before. We must all be willing to take another spin on the potter's wheel.

Paul's effort was to save Onesimus' life by changing Philemon's view of the situation. He was reaching deep into his heart to show Philemon that he had an issue. It is not enough to love those who love you, but we must learn to love those we do not know. I cannot imagine that Philemon knew the real Onesimus. Most slave masters would not take the time to fellowship that much with the hired help.

Therefore, in order to reach the "hired help," he would need to begin to show them, love. And, if they [the slaves] decided to give their hearts to the Lord, it could be that love drew them.

Questions:

- Do you welcome all newcomers to the church?

- What can you do to make new converts feel accepted?

- If you have never been led to show yourself friendly to new converts, pray and ask the Holy Spirit to help you see them and give you something to say.

STAGE SEVEN

This lesson verses: Phm 1:18-25

If he has done you any wrong or owes you anything, charge it to me. (Phm 1:18)

I, Paul, am writing this with my own hand. I will pay it back--not to mention that you owe me your very self. (Phm 1:19)

I do wish, brother, that I may have some benefit from you in the Lord, refresh my heart in Christ. (Phm 1:20)

Confident of your obedience, I write to you, knowing that you will do even more than I ask. (Phm 1:21)

And one thing more: Prepare a guest room for me, because I hope to be restored to you in answer to your prayers. (Phm 1:22)

Epaphras, my fellow prisoner in Christ Jesus, sends you greetings. (Phm 1:23)

And so do Mark, Aristarchus, Demas, and Luke, my fellow workers. (Phm 1:24)

The grace of the Lord Jesus Christ be with your spirit. (Phm 1:25)

DISCUSSION: WHEN ALL FAILS

It has been said many times, in society, "if all else fails," then do something different. And when we look at verses 18-21, we see that the Apostle Paul makes Philemon an offer that he could not turn down. He says, put the charge of what Onesimus owes on his account. This is what loves does; it covers the other person's sin.

When Jesus told the story of the Good Samaritan starting in Luke 10:30, he tells us that he did not pass the wounded man as the others did. He took pity; he bandaged the man's wounds, poured oil and wine upon his wounds, placed him on his donkey, and took him to an Inn. After taking care of him all night, he paid the innkeeper and asked that the innkeeper take care of this wounded man with a promise that if he does, whatever the cost incurred, he would reimburse him.

Jesus told this story so that he might answer the question, "who is my neighbor." Jesus was a great storyteller because he understood the hearts of men. He knew they would not accept the truth if he were direct, so he was gentle yet

153

firm. He told the story so each man could find themselves in the characters that chose to pass by rather than help. This particular man in the story wanted to make an excuse for how he would treat another person. The man knew what was right, for he quoted Jesus the law of loving God with all your heart, soul, strength, and mind. Then he added, love your neighbor as yourself. Although he knew the law, he did not truly abide by it. If he had, he would have never asked Jesus who is his neighbor.

To fully love is to <u>set no limits</u> on how you will treat another. Just as Jesus sets no boundaries on how he loves us, we, therefore, cannot impose restrictions either. If there had been a limit, Jesus would have died on the cross for a chosen few. But he decided to die for all.

The Apostle Paul, who is willing to pay Onesimus' debt, shows himself as the Good Samaritan. He was ready to go to any length to help Philemon's slave. I am sure that this act of love would hit Philemon right in the eye. Now Philemon is forced to reflect upon his heart. He would have to ask himself, "can I allow the Apostle to repay the debt, or should I let it go? He must consider how personal this letter is since the Apostle Paul is writing it. And finally, he would decide if he was going to obey this request. We can know the right thing to do in a situation and yet choose evil. And we can be put to shame when someone of caliber has such confidence in us that they force us to do the right thing. I wonder if the Apostle's confidence is his way of applying a little pressure on Philemon. Stating that his obedience will refresh his heart and to say how assured he is that Philemon will do the right thing is pressure.

My story version of the verse: 1:18-21

"When entering the thoughts of the Apostle Paul, I hear him thinking of a proper and perfect way to reach Philemon, so he writes. "If you are not able to release him from the wrong, he has caused you, charge it to me. I will take the responsibility of repaying you whatever the price you set."

"Onesimus is worth investing in, as I once invested in your Philemon. That is why I say that you owed me much. I will not elaborate on it any further because that would bring back up the past. I only speak of it now to remind you that you once stood in Onesimus shoes, and when you did, all were forgiven."

"I can forgive so easily, Philemon, because Christ has forgiven me far more than I can tell you. My past rises up and floods my mind with the hateful things that I once did. I remember the suffering that I caused the church. Believers who were in the Body of Christ suffered greatly because of me. I thought I was serving God by

155

getting rid of those who would not follow the law, but I came to learn that God was doing a new thing."

"I had to accept these people, and they had to accept me, the man who terrorized them. But God has forgiven me for my sins, and these experiences have taught me the power of forgiveness. It sets a man free and gives him a chance to start again, and that is what I want for you, Philemon. Yes, you, Philemon, I desire for you to have" harmony with Onesimus as I have peace with my brothers and sisters in Christ. I am now the Apostle of the Gentiles, the Apostle to the very people I harmed."

"If God can clean me up and remove my hatred, he can remove yours, Philemon. I thought you had to follow the law to please God, but I came to learn that there was a new law…a law of grace. It superseded the old one. Striking out against the new thing God was doing and not submitting to His will is like beating the sands in the desert with a stick. It does not ruin the sand nor change the composition of the dessert.

"We must put God first; we must walk in love if we are to understand what He is doing. Only through love will we be close enough to get a glimpse of what God is doing and an opportunity to participate. You think owning slaves is your right, and it is, but being a Christian requires you to expand your point of view. Are you willing to

156

let go of your rights so that God's plan comes to perfection?"

"I had to find out the hard way that the law is not God. It was a temporary method that included various rules that helped a man identify his sin(s). Then other men came along and added to the law and made it unbearable to live up underneath."

"Thank God for Jesus who came to get us all from up under the burden of the law? This is what you have to accept, Philemon; let go of your money pouch, stop counting coins for a man's life. He is far more valuable than that. And when you let go, then we can work on you about sharing the love of Christ to the untitled and unnamed people."

"I realize my fight with the Christian did not make our lives better, nor did it draw one Christian back into the traditions of our ancestors. Besides, the law could not save one soul from entering hell. It could only place them under the weight of its demand."

"Now, Philemon, it is your turn to accept new changes. Those changes were to better humanity. Is it not more important that everyone has the chance to receive Christ? Allow Onesimus and others like him to find their place in the Body if they wish to know our Savior. He will be please that you have torn down your idols and have allowed God to be exhausted in your life."

"My heart will be refreshed, knowing of your changes and your new choices. A Christian's life is full of sacrifices, my friend, but when we make those sacrifices from the heart, we find a blessing in the center of it."

"Did I tell you that I have confidence in you, Philemon? Since the day of your transformation, I have great hopes for what you will do. You started by opening up your home for the church to be established in Colossae. And now I am confident that you will open your heart once again."

"We shall be tried in this life over and over again, Philemon. And those testing will come in various forms. The pressure of life can become a burden, sometimes, but we know if we hold out and trust God, He will see us through it." "Let me warn you, my co-worker in the Lord; you are about to be tried again. Will you not open up your heart and allow the Love of Christ to enter, revive, renew, restore, build up, create, and produce more love in you? He is asking you to have a passion for those you have not considered before, and I think you will."

"Every man's servant and maiden under your ownership should be potential converts. Onesimus is just the first fruit that will come from your household. For this, I am confident that if you allow the Lord to bless you in a new way, it will come through your servants. I feel good in my soul that you will do the right thing, and "when a man's ways, please God," blessings are sure to follow." (105)

This lesson verses: Phm 1:22-25

> And one thing more: Prepare a guest room for me because I hope to be restored to you in answer to your prayers. (Phm 1:22)

> Epaphras, my fellow prisoner in Christ Jesus, sends you greetings. (Phm 1:23)

> And so do Mark, Aristarchus, Demas, and Luke, my fellow workers. (Phm 1:24)

> The grace of the Lord Jesus Christ be with your spirit. (Phm 1:25)

Discussion

We have come to the last four verses and the conclusion of our discussion
about them. The Apostle Paul tells Philemon in the closing of his letter that he hopes to come to visit soon. He requests a guest room to be ready for his arrival. He is confident that through the people's prayers that God would deliver him.

With Paul planning to visit, we must ask ourselves why. He is coming to see about his son Onesimus. Any father will try to stay connected to his adopted son and to encourage his growth. The other alternative is that he is coming to check on the church as he customarily does. And finally, he is coming to see Philemon and see how he is managing the entire situation with him and Onesimus.

The Apostle knows that this is a large task for Philemon, and therefore, he might need advice from him. Mostly, the Apostle wants to see, for himself, the new freedom that has come about for Onesimus as the two men work out their new relationship. And finally, the Apostle shares other personal greetings that came from other fellow servants of God.

My story version of verses: 1:22-25

"I am praying, Philemon, that all will work itself out, and it will because I know that you love the Lord. I am coming, and I am excited about what I will discover when I reach your home.
 I am especially excited about your character and how it is deepening in love. Your other brothers and servants of the Lord send their greetings to you: Epaphras, Mark, Aristarchus, Demas, and Luke. May the grace of our Lord Jesus Christ be with you."

Questions:

- Have you ever stepped up and protected Another person as the Apostle Paul was willing to do for Onesimus? (Read: Prov10:12, 17:9; Gal 6:10)

- Has anyone stepped in and paid a debt for you? (Read: Heb 10:18; Rom 13:8)

- Are you still walking in hatred and or unforgiveness? (Read: Matt 6:15)

- What are you willing to do to show that you have forgiven and are ready to move on with your life?

- Why did the Apostle Paul tell Philemon that he would visit when he is free from prison? Was he coming to visit or to spy on Philemon and Onesimus?

STAGE EIGHT

DISCUSSION: ON LOVE

As we walk out this Christian life, we never know when the Spirit will reveal to us a piece of our heart that needs to change. Sanctification is a process, and therefore, we are continuously evolving for the better.

We read in the scripture a set of instructions about relationships. We read that a man is to love his wife as Christ loves the church and that a wife must honor her husband. (106) As we continue to study out the Word of God, we learn that we are to love God with all our heart, soul, mind, and strength. (107)

In order to properly love God, our wives, and our husbands, we must first believe upon the name of Jesus Christ and his finished work. If we do, the love of Christ will live in us and cause us to love even further. We will learn to love our neighbors as ourselves and our wives as our flesh. If we obey these commandments and allow the Holy Spirit to help us, to love, it will openly demonstrate to the world that Christ dwells in us. (108)

Does your lifestyle reflect the love of Christ? Does it reflect it in every area of your life?

Philemon thought he loved; he had a church operating in his home, yet he needed to open his heart more to accept Onesimus.

You must see your love as a great net that casts itself out into the deep waters. Can you say it is wide enough to include all the different types of fish that live in the water? If you can honestly say no, "my net is not large enough," then you need to widen your net for a further reach.

Remember, if God so loved the world, and His Son, Jesus loved the world unto death, we have that same kind of love being heirs and joint-heirs with Christ and having the Father, Son, and the Holy Spirit dwelling inside of us.

You become love as God is love because God made provision for us to receive a new spirit. That new Spirit confirms that you are children of God. (109) If you find that you cannot forgive or you cannot accept someone for what they may have done, then try remembering when He accepted you and forgave you for your sins. God first loved you in your sins. (110) He loved you when you were unlovable and full of sin. Thus, we can work on ourselves to love those we see as unlovable.

With God's love flowing inside us and operating on the outside, we understand why the Apostle Paul wrote to Philemon. It was for the sake of his soul and the success of his ministry.

When was the last time you loved someone that you got involved in someone's situation to help resolve their problem? It cannot be denied; we really are our brother's keeper. (111)

We discover in Colossians 4:9 that the Apostle Paul references Onesimus again, but this time with a man named Tychicus. It tells us that the Apostle is sending the two men to the Christians in Colossae.

There is a strong belief that this Onesimus is the same person as in the book of Philemon. But it is not clear if Tychicus and Onesimus are taking the Philemon letter to Colossae or is this another occasion for Onesimus to return to Colossae. Could this be **our proof** that Philemon received the message from Paul, and now Onesimus is making a second trip as a liaison between the church in Colossae and the church in Rome? Amen!

STAGE NINE

DISCUSSION: FROM ROME TO HOME

Now Onesimus is on his way home. He and the Apostle Paul have hugged and said their goodbyes. Although Onesimus could travel alone, yet there is safety in numbers. I assumed that he traveled with a caravan that was on its way towards Colossae.

There is a lot of miles between Rome and Colossae, roughly 2110.0 kms or 1,311.09281 miles. (112) Every day, as they drew closer to Colossae, I am sure there were times he got a little concerned as he tried to anticipate Philemon's reactions.

How does a slave reconcile with his master? What does Onesimus have to offer that would be of value to lessen the punishment that was sure to come? He is not the old Onesimus, for that old man would not have voluntarily gone back home. The old man's nature of Onesimus would not be willing to humble himself before Philemon. But now, he is not ashamed of the gospel that lives inside him. That gospel tells him and tugs on him to submit to Philemon's authority.

He knows that he is no longer a slave to any man, but he would become one if it were to give glory to God. He would be the best slave possible so that his master [Philemon] and others could see that he does all things unto his Father, which is God, who sees everything.

At least, this is how I imagine he felt as he began his journey home. It can be hard sometimes to go back and set things right. Especially if your reason for running away is no longer entangled with your reason for coming home. Every bit of anger has left, including his reason for his anger. The Holy Spirit has brought peace to his soul.
In times of concern, I imagine that he would take out the letter Paul wrote on his behalf, and he would read it to regain his confidence. Especially on nights when his faith may not be solid as the rock his head was resting against. Oh, the questions that surely floated around inside his head.

Questions such as: (1) How shall I begin to apologize when I see Philemon? (2) How will I explain my reason for running? (3) How can I repay him for what I stole?

My story version of Concerns

"Oh God, be with me, for I have questions with no answers. How God shall I begin to apologize to my master, Philemon, when I see him? Is it best to start talking or allow him to speak first?" "And when it is my turn to speak, what do I say first? How do I tell him that when I left, I left as a poor-minded slave, useless to him, but now I have returned to him as a man of value? I now have convictions that rely on the principles of Jesus Christ and his finished work."

"I want to tell him I no longer see him as a threat or the head ruler who controls my life. You are the head of my life Lord. I want him to know that you have removed all hate and bitterness that I once held in my heart. Philemon is a fellow servant to the Most-High, and so am I. My identity rest in Chris and nowhere else."

"Yes, I acknowledge that he has ownership over me, but not as a slave in my mind. I have been set free. Not free to run again, but free to work as his servant until God sets me physically free. My vision is clear, and I know my purpose in life, and it does not conflict with my obligation to serve Philemon. I see and understand the difference between his ownership and God's ownership. Christ has set my mind and heart free, and one day he will set my body free. This freedom will not come by running away; or by any act of violence by me."

Then as Onesimus draws even closer to home, he lies down and looks at the stars as he once did when he was a slave on Philemon's land, but this

time the stars have a different effect upon him.
He begins to pray Isaiah 54:17:

"No weapon forged against me
shall prevail. For the Lord shall refute every
tongue that accuses me. This is my birthright as
a servant of the Lord.
You, O' God have promised this will be so."

DISCUSSION: 50 MILES

"When they are about fifty miles outside of
Colossae, he finds another method to comfort his
soul. He begins to sing unto the Lord. He
probably would have sung one of the Psalms, but
I feel this song is just as appropriate. Title: I
Look To You, Artist: R. Kelly"

As I lay me down
Heaven hears me now
I'm lost without a cause.
After giving it my all
Winter storms have come
And darkened my sun
After all that I've been through
Who on earth can I turn to?
I look to You, I look to You
After all my strength is gone
In You I can be strong
I look to You, I look to You

168

DISCUSSION: THE LAST NIGHT

Then the day arrives where Onesimus is right outside the city gate. I am sure that Satan was bombarding him with everything he had to get Onesimus to run again. Onesimus could even visualize himself running. But I believe something on the inside of Onesimus cried out to him. The Holy Spirit said, "Trust God," and Onesimus found the strength to get up that morning and walk into the city and onto his master's property.

He might have even walked up to his master's front door and knocked. If Onesimus' mind had not changed as to how he saw himself, he would not have come to the front door. He could still hear his old friends yelling, "Onesimus is back, Onesimus is back." He did not stop to converse with them; he needed to see Philemon's face. It was his eyes that would tell him if everything was going to be okay.

Then a servant opened the doors, and he began to yell, "Onesimus is back. He has come home." Philemon's family would scramble into the great hall. They would be amazed to find Onesimus at the door. Why, this would be a strange sight to see, where a slave returns home on his own! Then a door opened up on the left side of the great hall; its Philemon, coming out of the family library and their place of worship.

He stood in the opening of the door in his purple robe, and Onesimus walked over to him and bowed himself to the floor. He hands Philemon the letter from the Apostle. "Here, he said, this is from the Lord's servant, Apostle Paul." "What," said Philemon?"

'He quickly reached for it as the other family members drew closer to hear what the Apostle had written. Philemon had forgotten all about Onesimus bowed down on the floor; he began to read the letter."

"His facial expression changed as he read the letter, but no one knew how to interpret his expressions. Finally, his wife said, "Philemon, my love, please be so kind as to share the letter for all to hear unless it's personal or church business."

"Then Philemon began to read the letter aloud, and then they understood the various facial expressions he had made. Onesimus could not move from where he was. He remained bowed on the floor as he continued to pray to God for His mercy. When Philemon had finished the letter, everyone in the room began to praise God for the salvation of Onesimus. Onesimus could not believe his ears. He slowly looked up at Philemon, and he saw his eyes. They were full of joy. Then Philemon found his voice and spoke something like this:

170

MY VERSION OF THE REPLY

"My heart rejoices in the Lord, for today I recovered a servant who is now my brother, and God is pleased with him. The Apostle has placed his stamp of approval; thus, there is nothing more to say. "Rise up, man. You are not a slave but my brother! Come into the church and tell me all about Rome and the conditions that the Apostle is facing. Can we do anything to help with this matter of him being in prison in his home?"

"Onesimus begins to tell Philemon about the Apostle's situation. Philemon interrupts him, "Onesimus, closed the door." "We have work to do, he said." Philemon. The rest of the family looked at one another, and then they turned and went about their day.

Onesimus realized as he was closing the door that God had worked all things together for his good. He had also answered another important request, and his heart was at peace. For he now knows that <u>a man can change his stars</u>. He can be lifted out of slavery and negative thinking and placed into a life that appears impossible to have. He also recognized that this new life began with accepting Jesus as his Savior.

In his new life, he could count the blessings that had come to him. He is a child of God, son to the Apostle Paul and now a friend and brother to his master...Philemon. Can a slave reconcile with his master, or can a master settle with his slave? The answer is yes if the two absolutely love the Lord.

Faith is the foundation upon which our hopes are built upon. The evidence of things not seen. Rather, the conviction or persuasion of things not seen. Without faith, we would be limited to our senses only. (113) And the possibility to grow and expand ourselves would be stifled, **BUT GOD,** who can take an ordinary man and make him extraordinary.

Footnotes

1   Blue Letter Bible – Strong's
     Definition of Hope
2   David Cloud, Way of Life
     Literature, Azusa St, and the Birth
     of Pentecostalism - April 19,
     2016 - P.O. Box 610368, Port
     Huron, MI 48061- 866-295-
     4143,
     fbns@wayoflife.org   www.
     wayoflife.org/reports/azusa_street
     _and_the_birth_of_pentecostalism
3   Isa 55:8-9
4   1 Peter 2:9
5   Rom 9:11, 11:5, 11:7,11:28, 1
     Th 1:4; 2 Pe 1:10 6 2 Peter 1:3
7   Rom 8:14
8   Rom 8:14; 1 Jhn 3:1-2; Gal 3:26
9   Gal 3:14, 29, 13, Jhn 1:29; Heb 6:19,
     8:12,10:17; Jer 31:34, 32:40;
     Col1:12; Php 3:12, Ju 24; Rms
     8:39, 5:17, 8:31, 8:1. 2 Cor 5:21,1
     Jo 2:1, Tit 2;12, Ph 4:29 Jhn
     10:10;Eph 3:12, 1 Jhn
     5:4, Mk 16:17, Lu 10:19
10   1 Pe 3:12; Ps 91:15

Footnotes continue

11   Deu 28:3, 6
12   Jhn 16:13
13   Act 15:12, 14:3; Rom 15:19; 2 Co 12:12
14   Rom 8:11
15   Jhn 10:10
16   Zoe: The God-Kind of Life – Beautiful In Jesus"
     Beautifulinjesus.com/zoe-god-kind-Life/
17   Eze 37:5
18   Rom 10:17
19   Matt 19:23, 26
20   1 King 19:19 21 2 Sam 13:1, 22-30 Sam 14:33, 2 Sam 15:1-6, 2 Sam 18:1- 182 Convert Unit
     Converunits.com/from 211+miles/to/km
23   2 Samuel 1:17-27
24   Matt 26:15
25   Phil 4:19
26   Rom 5:8
27   Eph 3:5
28   Eph 3:6
29   Rom 5:6
30   Jhn 15:7
31   Jhn 15:16; 16:23
32   Jas 1:6
33   Roman Culture
     Thirdmill.org/paul/roman_culture.asp
34   Acts 28:16

Footnotes continue

35 1 Th 1:3
36 Prov 16:19, 29:23; Isa 57:15
37 1 Jhn 1:19
38 Rom 8:33; Tit 1:1
39 Eph 1:5
40 Acts 9:10-17
41 Luk 10:19
42 Luk 10:20
43 Jas 1:2-4
44 Heb 12:1
45 Jas 1:19
46 What is Hope www.spirthome.com
     /hope.htm
47 Heb 11:1 48
48 Jhn 14:13-14, 16:26,
     15:16; Jhn 16:23-24
49 Job 2:13
50 Acts 12:5-9
51 Acts 19:23-40
52 Acts 8:27-38
53 Phil 2:3
54 Phil 2:4
55 Phil 2:5
56 Phil 2:7
57 Phil 2:8
58 Isa 53:12
59 Rom 14:11; Phi 2:11
60 Acts 8:27-28-31
61 Acts 8:36
62 Jhn 8:35
63 1 Co 7:21

Footnotes continue

64 Gal 3:8
65 Col 3:11
66 Eph 6:5
67 Eph 6:9
68 Phm 1:2
69 Phm 1:2
70 Phm 1:8
71 1 Jhn 3:10
72 Psa 139:23-24; 51:10
73 2 Cor 10:5
74 Blue letter Bible – Strong's G1108
    Knowledge
75 Jas 1:19; Eph 4:26
76 Matt 6:14
77 Gal 5:22-23
78 2 Cor 5:17
79 The Greek meaning of the name
    Onesimus: beneficial, profitable.
    Behindthename.com/name/onesimus
    The Hebrew "will be useful," The
    Etymology: "to be of use or to
    profit- www.abarim-publications.com
    /Meaning/Onesimus.html
80 Rom 4:17
81 Gen 1:27; 5:2
82 Psa 139:13-16
83 Acts 13:1-13
84 Acts 13:1-2
85 Acts 13:13
86 Acts 15:36-41
87 Acts 15:39-40
88 Deu 32:30
89 2 Tim 4:11